Shadow Light

Beautiful Beings #3

kailin gow

Shadow Light: Beautiful Beings Book 3

Kailin Gow

DEDICATION

To my teachers and friends at Sacred Heart School for filling my head with a lifetime of great gothic private school experiences.

Prologue

It All Begins Again

A week had passed since Shayne had been taken away and the portal opened, but we still had no idea where the portal could be. I'd spent hours with Brax, and a few nights with Asher looking in and around San Francisco. As talented as they were, and as trained as I was as a demon slayer, we had no luck.

"If Dr. Kingsley were here, we'd have no problem finding the portal," Moore said.

The halls of St. James Academy were filled with easy going, carefree students who had no idea about the hell we were going through.

I glanced at Moore as we meandered through the sea of students on the way to my locker. I knew he wanted to find this portal as much as I did, and though he'd deny it,

I had a feeling he wanted to find Shayne as well. Though he'd grown estranged from his sister, I knew he still loved her.

"I spent all afternoon with Braxton a few days ago," I said. "We went through every desk drawer, every filing cabinet and found nothing. We even flipped through his books. Do you know how many books he has?"

Moore nodded in understanding.

"Hundreds."

"So you spent the afternoon with Braxton, huh?"

Every time Braxton's name came up I saw a change in Moore's expression, in his mood, and in his attitude. He knew the last week had been all business. It'd been a rush to find the portal. There was no reason for him to get jealous or suspicious.

"I think we have no choice but to keep our eyes and ears open. We have to stay on the look out for the slightest activity."

Moore looked down the hall, his gaze darting from one attractive student to the next. "This is probably the first place we'll notice any kind of activity, but we've only got four pairs of eyes, and there are hundreds of students here."

"Don't worry," I said as we reached my locker. "We're more alert than mere mortals. If something is happening, we'll know."

He set a warm and friendly kiss on my brow. "I'll see you later."

For a long and leisurely moment I watched his long lean legs carry him away and sighed. He was so unbelievably beautiful with his blonde hair that curled slightly to the nape of his neck and dark blue eyes.

I yanked my locker door open, dumped my biology books over the pile that'd been tossed on the floor earlier that morning, and grabbed my gym clothes. The sound of pounding footsteps caught my attention and I immediately went on high alert, only to see Asher speed down the intersecting hall in hot pursuit of a diminutive demon.

Neglecting to close my locker and letting my gym clothes fall to the floor, I ran after him, eager to get my hands on any demon who might give us insight into the whereabouts of the portal. By the time I caught up with Asher, he was ducking into the boys' locker room. Without wasting any time checking whether guys were changing or not, I shoved the door open and bulldozed my way in.

Though my focus immediately went to Asher at the far end of the locker room, I could see the dozens of young men in various states of undress. On any other day I might have ventured a selfish glimpse, but today, my sole goal was helping Asher get that demon.

To the left of me, in my periphery, through the mass of skin, sweat and muscles I caught a flash of movement, a familiar figure... Asher.

"Hey, Lux," a jock called out. "Want to join our lacrosse team?"

I offered him a wry grin, managed to keep my gaze above the belt and backed out to wait for Asher in the hall. No doubt he'd prefer to take care of business once the guys had cleared the locker room. I paced impatiently in front of the door. This was the first demonic activity we'd seen since that night with Shayne. It was important we catch it. It was important we question it.

The door swung open and I prepared for battle, but instead of facing Asher, I turned to see Braxton, looking very pale but preoccupied.

"Brax." Had he been one of the semi nude guys cleaning up after the game? "Did you see Asher in there?"

The blank stare on Braxton's face scared me. I'd never seen him so out of sorts.

"Braxton, did you hear me?" We'd not seen each other since our meeting in his uncle's office. Had he been in this trance since then?

"Yeah," he muttered. "I heard you. I didn't see Asher. I don't even remember going into the locker room to begin with."

I grabbed his shoulders and redirected him to the door of the locker room. "We have to go in there and find Asher. I'll give you thirty seconds to go in and warn those guys to cover up, then I'm coming in."

"Those guys?" He looked at me, clueless.

"The lacrosse team just got off the field and they're all in there showering and changing. I want to give them a decent chance to cover up before I barge in again."

"Lux?" For the first time his eyes registered a faint sign of recognition. Time stopped for a moment as he leaned in and looked closely at me, almost looking inside me. His gaze flickered with pain, with memories and with love.

"I need your to help now, Braxton," I said softly but with firm determination. "Will you go in there now?"

He reached for my hand and fingered my palm. "Sure, Lux. I'll help you. I'll go in."

Despite his words, he made no move to go into the locker room.

"Now, Brax?" I gave him a gentle nudge toward the door.

"Yeah," he mumbled with a vague nod. "Yeah, now."

He disappeared into the locker room and thirty seconds later I went in, ready or not. The guys had covered up and many were ready to leave. Brax and I strolled through the rows of lockers while a few remaining stragglers slowly got their things together and prepared to leave.

"What exactly are we looking for?" Brax asked.

Hearing the flow of water from the showers, I led him to the stalls at the far end of the locker room. Steam rose and the heat was suddenly stifling. Braxton stopped, reluctant to enter the heated mist. I forged on ahead of him, checking in every stall and finding each of them empty. When I reached the source of the steaming water I could barely see into the stall.

My hand to the crucifix at my neck I took a step into the stall. The water was far too hot for any human to tolerate. But…

I reached in and turned the hot water off. "Oh my God."

"What is it, Lux?"

Sickened and angry, I leaned against the damp ceramic wall and stared at the drained and empty shell of a young male student. I didn't want Braxton to see this, not now. He seemed already so fragile as it was. Seeing a lifeless and soulless teammate was not what he needed. "Nothing… just the heat that's so intense."

"I hear something from over there," Braxton called.

Hurrying to his side, I tried to capture the sound he heard. A faint muffled sound came from the second row of lockers. "Come on." The muffled sound became clearer until we reached a dented locker.

Braxton reached for the latch and pulled the locker open.

"Ah," Asher cried as he fell out of the cramped locker. "It's about time you came around. Man, do you know what it's like to be squeezed in between dirty socks and a damp jock strap?"

"Sorry." I tried to sound as sympathetic as I could, but had trouble biting back on a giggle. "You disappeared." I looked around for signs of a struggle, of a fight.

"I was about to faint in there."

"What happened to the demon? How d'you get in to the locker?"

Asher glared at Brax. "It's him."

"Braxton?"

"He shoved me in here." He glanced over his shoulder at a tear in his shirt. "Damn near scraped my shoulder off in the process. These things aren't meant to fit a big guy like me."

I turned to Braxton, reluctant to accuse him, but with no other choice. "Brax, did you really do this?"

He frowned and looked into the locker. "I didn't," he said with a shake of his head. "I would never do something like that."

"Well, I never thought you'd be able to manage it either, but... hell, you shoved me in there as if I were five foot two and barely fifty pounds. The demon flew right past you. Is that why you shoved me in here?"

"I don't know," Brax said with a shrug. "I don't even remember seeing you in here."

"Well, think about it. By shoving me in there you let the demon get to a soul."

"Bobby." Braxton's voice droned on, lifeless and dull. "Bobby Fleishman."

I stared at him and tried to figure out how he knew. He couldn't possibly have seen him from where he'd stood.

His skin turned ashen and for a moment I thought he was going to be sick right there. "He's in the shower, drained."

It didn't make sense. If what Asher said was true, Braxton had actually aided a demon. He helped the demon capture and drain Bobby, yet he couldn't remember any of it.

No, I suddenly thought. I moved in closer to Braxton and felt a quick sense of desire take over me. I'd always been attracted to Brax, but this was different. This was intense and the attraction I now had for him permeated my whole body. It took every ounce of determination and will to pull away from him.

His incubi side had become stronger.

"What are you guys trying to say?" Braxton's brow furrowed as his confusion turned to frustration and anger. "You guys think I'm responsible for Bobby's death?"

Wanting to sooth and calm him, I reached for his hand. "We have to find a way to break the curse, Brax, fast."

"No, it's not what you think. I'm not some monster who would allow a friend, a teammate to be…" He looked at me with wild eyes. "You're wrong."

"I'm not, Brax. You just can't see it anymore, but the curse is taking over."

Reason penetrated through the blur that'd taken over his brain and he squeezed my hand. "I hate this," he muttered. "But maybe you're right."

"Don't worry. We'll find a way."

"Yeah," he muttered as he brought his palm to his forehead. "I don't even know who I am anymore."

Chapter 1

The Book of Angels

Very quietly the police came and cordoned off the boys' locker room, but no announcement was made regarding Bobby's death. It was as though nothing had happened. We had to go on with our classes as if everything was normal. It was so strange, but it appeared they didn't want to create a mass panic at school, which would cause parents to pull their children out.

When class finally let out, I wanted to scream for the frustration of it all. A boy had died and I felt useless and helpless. I dumped my books in my locker and hurried out, eager to get home before Asher arrived.

He'd gotten into the habit of coming over for dinner every Thursday, something my mom loved.

"He's all alone and deserves to have a minimal sense of family after the ordeal he went through," she'd said. "I can't believe his parents didn't even bother coming into town after his little stint in jail."

I loved her all the more for accepting him.

As I thought of him, I saw him in the distance, sexy and dangerous as he straddled a low riding Harley wearing a black t-shirt that hugged him like a second skin and a leather bomber jacket that added to his broad shoulders and chest. It was hard to believe Mom saw him as a helpless little boy who needed a hot meal and convivial conversation on a regular basis. To everyone else who saw him, he was strong, almost arrogant and unapproachable.

"Hey," I said as I came up to him. "Since when do you stay until the last class?"

"Ever since another attack happened. I wanted to stick around and make sure you were okay."

"Thanks. I'm fine."

"Want to hop on?"

I felt the involuntary grimace that came to my face and hoped Asher hadn't noticed.

"What," he said with a smirk. "Are you afraid of getting on a motorbike?"

"Of course not." I set my hands on my hips and glanced at the narrow little seat behind him.

"It'll get you home a lot faster. Come on, Miss Slayer. We don't have much time to waste."

I knew he was right. "Fine." Grabbing a hold of his shoulders with one hand, I gathered my pleated navy blue skirt and swung my leg over and snuggled up behind him.

"That school uniform has never looked better. Nothing says sexy like a school uniform on a Harley."

"I'm sure the people of St. James would be delighted to hear that."

I wrapped my arms around him and squeezed.

"Hmm, I could get used to this."

Loosening my hold, I said, "Just drive already."

He glanced over his shoulder, reached back for my hand and pulled it tightly across his hardened abs. "The roads can get a little bumpy, so you gotta hang on."

Whatever fear and trepidation I felt at the thought of riding a motorcycle disappeared the moment I set my head to his shoulder. Warmth exuded from him and I felt safe.

"I'll hang on if it makes you feel better, but even if I did fall off the bike, I know you'd be there to catch me, wouldn't you, my Guardian?"

The bike roared out of the parking lot, thundering past Porsches, BMWs and Jaguars that purred in tame comparison.

"Always and forever," Asher said.

Though his voice was lost in the roar of his bike, I still managed to hear the soft and potent promise.

Before long, he turned down my street. Looking at the picture perfect houses, lined up in pretty colors, with pretty shutters and pretty gingerbread trims... it was almost impossible to believe the ugliness that lay in the city's underbelly.

"Told you I'd get you home fast."

"And safe. Thanks."

He'd become so familiar with my home, that he didn't wait for me to let him in, but he just walked in as if he'd always lived there.

"Hi, Mom," I called out.

The house smelled of cookies and breads, the perfect homecoming after an ugly day at school.

"When did you have so much time to bake? Weren't you at work today?" Mom was a director at the museum at Golden Gate Park. She wasn't the baking cookies type, but since Asher began coming over, she became more motherly. He had that effect on women, and for me at first when I met him. With his ink black hair and blue eyes, and the way he always looked at me; I wished I felt the same about him as he did for me.

"I went in early this morning, took care of a few things and decided to come home early. You kids have a nice day in school?"

"Let's just say a nice homemade meal with nice folks is going to be the perfect end to this day."

"Precisely what I like to hear. Dinner will be ready in an hour."

"Great," I said. "Thanks, Mom."

"I look forward to another great meal, Mrs. Collins."

I could have sworn Mom blushed.

I led Asher up the narrow staircase to my room. A brief wave of embarrassment swept through me as I caught sight of the tornado that'd passed through my room. I'd neglected my room for days and was loathed to ask my mother to pick up for me. Clothes I'd worn the week before still lay on the floor and three pairs of shoes mingled together in a pile by the closet door.

None of this bothered Asher much. As soon as we were alone with the door closed, he pulled me into his arms.

"Asher." I set my hand to his chest, but he pushed on and kissed me. "Asher," I protested. "What's gotten into you?"

"I don't know," he muttered softly as his lips brushed across my cheeks. "With everything that's been going on… I feel…"

I leaned my brow to his, wanting to understand, but knowing it was wrong for us to be together. "Asher, you're my guardian. We can't."

"Nothing's been confirmed yet. I may be your guardian. I may not. As far as I'm concerned, I'm just a normal everyday guy, who is really and truly attracted to an extraordinary girl. Lux, I can't help what I feel for you, guardian or not. I felt this way even before this whole guardianship began."

"Well," I said as I patted his muscular chest. "You certainly are sweet."

"Don't let the secret out."

"Right. Wouldn't want to dent your bad boy image." Although I tried to be playful, I could still see the intensity in his eyes.

"Look, I just want to take my chances while I still can. You haven't made a commitment to Braxton or Moore. I have to at least take a chance and try to persuade you to consider me."

Chuckling softly, I ran my hands over the breadth of his shoulder and down his arms. Even through his leather jacket I could feel the power and strength harbored there. Sweet, yes, I thought, but oh so dangerous and strong when called for. He was my new guardian, who turned out to have angel blood in him. He was also the bad boy of St. James Academy, who was staring at me with his intense blue eyes, willing me to take a chance with him. "Lux, we're going to be together a lot, and this...being this close is going to be the hardest thing for me, as your guardian or even being one of your demon slayers." He touched my cheek gently, his thumb grazing the bottom of my lips. I closed my eyes because I did feel an attraction to him.

I knew I had a connection to Asher, just as I did to Moore and Braxton. Fate had brought us all together, just as it had brought me to my destiny as a demon slayer when I was two years old.

Asher sighed and pulled back. With a faint grunt of resignation, he shoved his fingers through the thick dark waves of his hair, raking stray locks off his face. "I knew it wouldn't be easy, but, hey, I had to try, right?"

"I guess."

"But, I promise you, when all of this is said and done, you'll realize that Moore is not what you need, and Braxton is not what you want." He looked at the ground and back up at me. "It'll only break your heart Lux. Now that you know what they are, and what we are."

"Time will tell. We'll just have to wait and see," I said with a teasing grin.

"We might end up seeing you slaying one of them... or both."

Frowning, I glared at him, virtually daring him to explain himself. His grin faded, but he said nothing in his defense.

"Let's move on to more serious business." I turned to my grandmother's special chest and turned the key. "Good thing I at least have this safely tucked away."

Asher smiled as I pulled out the thick and heavy Book of Angels and plopped it down on my bed. With a boyish grin and playful cock of his brow, he fell back onto the bed.

"A little night time reading?" He patted the book.

My cheeks heated up, and I couldn't understand why I was so flustered. "I've been reading a lot about angels lately. I'm almost finished with another one I have, but need your help with this one. I'm curious and want to know as much as I can. Hopefully in all this I'll also be able to find out what I am."

He reached for my hand and held my fingers tenderly in his. "I know you've been going through a rough time lately. I know how difficult it is to wake up one day and realize you're not what you thought. It takes some getting used to."

"I know, and to a large extent I appreciate and accept whatever it is that I am, but I want to know. I want some confirmation."

"Look, I've been there. I've asked the questions you're asking and I've had the doubts and confusion. I also went through a phase of anger and resentment, something you'll probably go through after this first phase fizzles."

"Great," I said with a sarcastic smirk. "Give me something to look forward to."

"Just know that I'll be there for you, no matter what happens, and no matter what you find out."

I sat beside him and looked at the length of his stretched out form. I pulled the heavy book onto my lap. "Thanks. I already knew that, but it's good to hear all the same."

In that moment I wanted nothing more than to stretch out along side of him, to feel the warmth of his body and to just curl up in the safety of his arms. Looking at him, I couldn't resist reaching out to run my fingers through his hair. The thick dark waves were soft and alluring.

"You certainly are a handsome guardian, aren't you?"

"I think that's the first time you've actually come out and complimented me."

"Naw," I said with a smile. "I'm sure I've told you before." I curled a lock around my thumb.

"No, you never have. I'd remember."

"Well, then, I'm telling you now. I'd admire you Asher, not only for your looks and strength, but there's

- 23 -

something free about you. You don't seem to care what people think and you go ahead and do what you what you want with no apologies."

"I wasn't always so confident, Lux," he said evenly, "but there comes a time when you realize you have to be your true self. You can't live your life based on what others expect of you. I sure got that message when I realized my parents would never really be happy with my choices, no matter what. So I decided to let them be unhappy with me, all the while making sure I was happy with me."

"Did your art help you?"

He shrugged. "A means to express yourself is always good. I guess you could say that I vent my soul through my drawings. A few years back I painted something so ugly and raw, so painful to look at, I realized it was the fear and uncertainty I felt inside that had come out through my brush, and through my choice of colors."

"Maybe I should take up painting."

"Why not? I'd be more than happy to give you a few private lessons."

I let out an amused snort and ruffled his hair. "Yeah, can you just imagine it? The rebel tough guy tutoring the demon slayer in, what, of all things? Art."

My gaze fixed on his torso, on the tightness of his t-shirt and when I met his eyes I knew it was going to be hard staying out of his arms. We were so similar in so many ways, and I knew I could learn so much from him by spending more time with him.

"How 'bout you start by tutoring me in Latin." I flipped through the thick yellowed pages of the Book of Angels. Each page was crisp and dry, threatening to crack if pulled back too far. Even the scent spoke of ages. "Was Latin a natural part of your transformation? I mean, did you just automatically understand it, or did you have to learn?"

"Ha, nothing comes that easy. No I had to learn, and I had to work hard to learn. I'll admit I'm not the greatest student, but really, Latin is not easy."

I frowned and felt defeated before I'd even begun.

"You need a hand understanding something in there?" He sat up and looked over my shoulder at the book.

"I went online and picked up a few words and I get the gist of some of this, but there's so much. I can't keep up. Every time I find enough words to get by on, I come across a whole new batch of words and turn of phrases that I don't understand."

"Let's take a look. What, exactly are you hoping to find in here?"

"A way to break the curse that was put on Brax and Moore."

He looked at me and bit his lip, and for a moment I thought he'd refuse to help me. "I don't know if something like that would be in a book like this." He took the book from my hands and carefully turned the pages. "But we'll take a look."

"Hey, Lux! Asher!" Mom called from downstairs.

I left Asher's side and went to the top step of the stairs. "What is it?"

"Your dad just called. I'm going to go meet him for dinner. We're going to meet the replacement for Dr. Kingsley... a Dr. Fitzpatrick."

"Fine, Mom. Don't worry about dinner. I'll fix something."

"Well, at least you'll have fresh baked cupcakes for dessert."

"Thanks, and have a good time."

I turned to get back to Asher and the Book of Angels, but instead of hearing my mother walk out the door, I heard her come up the stairs. I grabbed the book from Asher's hands, threw it on the bed and tossed a cushion over it.

After a quick rap on the door, Mom pushed it open and popped her head in. "Hey, Asher. I know it's Thursday and I'd promised you a home cooked meal, but I do have to run."

He stood and went to kiss her cheek. "That's fine, Mrs. Collins. I already appreciate everything you do for me." He held her hands in his. "I haven't eaten so well since… well, I really can't remember when."

"It's always a pleasure to have you Asher, and I promise, I'm going to make it up to you tomorrow. How does lasagna sound?"

"Perfect. I already look forward to it. And don't worry about dinner tonight. I'll help Lux whip up some great homemade smoothies. I'm not just a pretty face you know. I am handy in the kitchen."

"I don't doubt it," Mom patted his cheek.

"That'll be perfect," I added. "So we'll have something homemade after all. Practically gourmet."

She came to give me a hug. "Sorry I have to run off like this, but your Dad is waiting for me. There's some dinner or something to welcome the new dean."

"Yeah, I heard," I said with a nod. "Have fun, Mom."

"I will, honey, but don't you kids have too much fun."

"Don't worry, we won't. We have a lot of studying to do."

"Great." She kissed my forehead and turned to head for the door. "I'll see you later."

Asher and I gazed at one another as we listened to her go downstairs, gather her purse and keys and walk out. Only then did Asher speak up.

"She doesn't know?"

"No, neither of them knows." I returned to sit on the bed and pulled the Book of Angels out from its hiding place. "I haven't been able to find the way to tell them I'm sprouting wings. How do I explain that to them, especially since they don't have any? Where did I get it from?"

He sat beside me and pulled me into his arms. "Don't worry. Things'll work out. At least you have open and honest communication with them. I'm sure when you're ready to talk, they'll be ready to listen. You're really lucky, you know. Your parents are great. I can't even begin to imagine having such understanding parents."

"That may be true, but I still want to keep them out of this. They've already been through so much, watching me grow up as a demon slayer. I think I want to spare them at least the questioning and uncertainty I'm going through. I'll tell them about this when I know what *this* is."

"Who knows, maybe they already know. They're pretty smart. I don't think my parents ever knew, granted they weren't around much to notice there was something different about me. Honestly, I think they wouldn't have seen a thing even if they'd stayed with me for any amount of time."

"I'm sorry you had to do so much growing up on your own."

He hugged me tighter and kissed my temple. "Forget about all that. Despite everything, I'm grateful; grateful for what I have now. Finding you was a big relief. I needed to find someone who was just like me."

He cupped my chin and turned me to look at him. His eyes, so often hard and uncompromising, were now soft and warm, welcoming me into his sphere, into his world. I knew this was important to him.

"You have no idea how happy I am that I found out about you. It's answered so many questions about myself. It's helped me understand so much more about my life."

"You know, I glad too."

Chapter 2

Ethereal Sight

Asher's knowledge of Latin proved inadequate as we flipped through the Book of Angels. He'd managed to pick up on a few words here and there.

"I'm going to have to look some of this up again," he'd said as he scratched his head. He pointed to a line. "Bellum, that means war, but basium... that's a kiss."

"The kiss of war."

"Then you have hostium, or enemy, but here you have amicitia, which is friendship."

"One extreme to the other."

"Yeah. And here you have abisco, which could mean to split or separate."

The words spun around in my head as I headed to Brax's door after dinner. Asher had to head back home so I arrived at the Kingsley mansion by myself. I'd hope to arrive with an answer to the curse he lived with and to check up on him, especially how he had been so shaken by this morning's demon incident. Without much progress with the Book of Angel, I felt empty and useless. Despite that, I had to see him. His parents had asked me to protect him, and I still cared deeply for him as a friend and something more.

"Lux," he answered with a distinctive lack of enthusiasm when he opened the door. If anything his voice held a heavy tone of despair and darkness.

"Hey," I said lightly. "Can I come in?"

Scrutinizing me, he hesitated a moment, then pulled open the door without a word.

The big mansion was even more silent and void of life than when his uncle was alive. Brax had mentioned letting some of the help go, not so much for financial reasons, but simply to have more privacy.

He led me to his uncle's library, a room he had adopted and spent much time in.

"Brax," I said as I sat down. "Just to ease your mind, I don't really think you had anything to do with what happened to Bobby. I don't think you're the one who drained him."

"That's good to hear." His voice remained cool and unmoved, just as he did. He stood, stiff and still beside me. "But it doesn't really answer much though. I mean, I don't even remember going into the locker room to begin with. I didn't play lacrosse today because I was behind on an essay I had to write for English Lit, and I'd spent an hour at the library. I had no reason to go to the gym."

"And the gym and library are practically at opposite ends," I said.

"That and I don't understand why I would shove Asher into a locker. It doesn't make sense."

"I know how frustrating all this must be for you, but we'll find out what's really going on and we'll find a way to break you from this curse." I reached out for his hand and gave a gentle tug, hoping to incite him to sit beside me. Though he didn't quite pull his hand from mine, he did resist the tug toward the chair. "Asher and I have been pouring over the Book of Angels hoping to find something that would help. So far we haven't found anything concrete; something about friends and enemies, about love and war."

"You're wasting your time. You guys can't help me."

"Don't say that, Brax. You can't give up. Remember what your parents said. You need an angel's help."

He gazed down at me, his eyes vague and unsure.

I gave his hand a teasing squeeze. "So now we know I have some angel blood in me. I guess that's why I was so drawn to you right from the start."

The Braxton I'd come to know finally broke through. He grinned. "It's not simply because you found me attractive?"

I gave his hand a playful slap and leaned back into my chair. "You? Atrractive?"

He sat on the edge of his uncle's desk and clasped his hands over his lap. "Some girls happen to think I'm attractive."

It was good to see him back to his old self.

"I guess you could say that I'm not like some girls."

"Oh, you could definitely say you're not like some girls. In fact you like no other girl I've ever met. You're Lux, and unique in so many ways."

"You're just saying that because I want to save you that's all."

"And I know you'll do it." It was his turn to reach out for my hand. He pulled me out of my chair and pulled me to him. He was so vulnerable in that moment, I wanted to wrap my arms around him and tell him everything would be okay. That I would be there for him, especially now.

But, as he tried to bring me closer, I kept a safe distance from him, refusing to come into his embrace. "Hold on, Brax."

"I thought you…"

"You know, I'm still a little mad at you."

"Mad? At me? I thought you said you didn't think I had anything to do with what happened to Bobby."

"Not that, Brax. Your confession that day at Yosemite… about your relationship with Shayne."

Shaking his head, he pulled me closer. "I'm sorry about that. I know I should have told you about it sooner… before you learn about it the way you did. Lux, that whole thing with Shayne was a long time ago, and honestly, I never really gave it much thought. I was lost, she was there, then, before you knew it, I was not there. It was really as quick as that. I met her, got to know her and moved on. Now, can we move on?"

"It's not the fact that you guys have this history together, it's the fact that you didn't tell me yourself. You know you had plenty of chances to do so, but you said nothing. I can't help but wonder what else you might be hiding."

"I wasn't hiding it, Lux. I just didn't think it was that important because she didn't mean anything to me. Look Lux, I'll tell you stuff about me then. I'll be open and honest to you. What do you want to know? I never told you I broke my arm when I was six years old. I climbed onto the counter to get my favorite cereal bowl and fell off. When I was nine I had a paper route. My parents had grounded me and cut my allowance and I wanted to go to the movies with a friend. So I collected my paper route money from my clients, pocketed the money and went to the movies."

"Brax..."

"Then when I was twelve my best friend and I decided to bike out into the county side to camp. Our backpacks were full of canned soup, canned fruits and canned tuna. By the time we arrived at our destination, we were so exhausted we called his father and had him come pick us up."

"That's enough, Brax. You know very well that this is different."

"Of course, relationships. Well, how about this? I went to Italy when I was fifteen and met a girl there, Becca. For the whole two weeks I was there, I spent every minute I could with her. I was heartbroken when I came back, but, hell, two weeks later I was hanging with my friends and Becca was just a cool memory from a really cool vacation. Is there anything else you want to know?"

"I knew Shayne. I hung out with Shayne."

"You hung out with her brother."

"You know this is more than a simple omission. You knew this would matter."

Brax swallowed and cast his gaze to the hardwood floor. "It wasn't intentional. If anything, you have to believe it wasn't intentional. I mean, maybe, somewhere in the back of my head I was afraid to tell you. Maybe I was afraid how you'd react, but I didn't intentionally mean to deceive you or hide anything from you."

I looked at him, silent as I thought through everything he'd said.

"You know how Shayne can be when she makes up her mind. She came on strong, and I gave in. Not exactly the kind of thing I'm proud of and go around telling new girls I meet."

"New girls?"

"You know what I mean… you." A hint of a grin came to his lips. "Come on, Lux. Don't tell me that I've lost you forever just because of a stupid thing like this."

"I'm here, aren't I?"

"Yeah." He bit his bottom lip in that adorable way he had. "You are."

I stepped closer and but not enough to allow him to wrap me in his arms. "Brax, I care so much for you, you have no idea. I don't have many friends. When I was brand new, you stepped in and showed me around St. James. You're one of my closest friends."

"Ouch." He winced and pulled back. "Friends?"

"Brax, this isn't the time to get wrapped up in emotions. I'm here to help you, and Asher's doing everything he can to help, too. For now I want you to put your energy towards controlling yourself."

He snickered. "Controlling myself?" With a firm yank, he pulled me into his arms. "How about controlling *yourself?*"

I felt the pull right away; the attraction, the arousal, the desire. It was strong and overpowering, making it almost impossible to control myself. My limbs were suddenly leaden and unable to pull away. I leaned into him, wanting to lose myself in his embrace, in his kiss.

My God, his lips were so tempting. They looked soft and inviting and I could already smell the enticing scent of his breath.

"Brax, I just came here to..." My voice was unusually husky, heavy with sexual tension and with the strain of holding back. "I came to help you."

"Then help me." His voice was just as heavy with desire as mine. He leaned in to brush his lips against my temple, and I closed my eyes, waiting for him to move his lips down to mine. My hunger for him was overwhelming, and I wrapped my arms around his neck, pulling him closer.

Before his lips found mine, I came to my senses.

"Brax, I can't. Not like this. This pull…I mean I'm want you, but now as strong as this… it's like I want you to devour me, to take me."

Brax smiled. "That good?" He leaned in again.

I pushed him away and said, "Remember how whenever we kissed when we first dated, I kept seeing Moore's face? I kept feeling this strong desire for him, although I was with you? It was like an enchantment."

Brax ran his hand through his hair and let out a sigh of frustration. "I remember that alright," he said gruffly. "I didn't like it one bit, and I wanted to protect you from him."

"But now your incubi powers are giving you that same ability as Moore's. You're irresistible, and I want more or you. I want you to do more than what I should be doing. You're using your power over me."

"No," he shouted. His hands were strong and firm as he gripped my hips and held me at arms' length. "Damn it."

"Brax, I know you're not intentionally trying to control me, but you have to be careful."

"I can't believe this. I'm already going through so much, and on top of it all, you're now telling me that I have the power to draw you to me, but that very power is what is now repelling you. I'm using all my will power, every ounce of discipline to keep from ravishing you, but all you want is…"

He stood and walked to the window, plowing his hands through his hair then balling his fists and pounding the air in front of him.

"Please, Brax. I hate to see you upset like this. I'm doing everything I can to get you out of this curse, but you have to be patient."

Looking at him now, it was almost impossible to see the handsome and strong young man I met just a few months ago. He'd been virtually flawless; his fair hair in shimmering curls around his face, his smile, alluring in its boyish appeal, his build, strong, powerful and so sexy.

These past days, I'd watch him crumble before my eyes. His was a soft, deteriorating shell of his former self.

"I thought we had something together," Brax murmured, his eyes staring blankly out the window.

"Brax, those days we spent together, all those nights you tutored me, helped me… got me through tests, quizzes and exams, I really did have a good time with you. I enjoy your company. You're a smart and funny guy…"

"But…"

I thought of the few long and lingering kisses we'd shared. He was so perfect in so many ways, yet… Why didn't I feel that… that special something, that spark? Where were the butterflies and damp palms?

With my heart aching, I reached for him, hoping to transmit the affection, however platonic it might be, to him. But the gentle touch of my hand to his shoulder wasn't received as platonically as it had been delivered.

Brax turned to me, pulled me possessively into his arms and lowered his lips over mine. Hard and determined, he pried my lips apart with his tongue and reached in to taste my tongue. It felt like heaven, and I let out a low moan. He tightened his hold on me. He was almost savage in his embrace. His fingers dug into the flesh of my back, up my shoulders and through my hair. Tightening his grip, he held me close, while he deepen his kisses.

"Brax," I shouted, finally able to pull back and push him away.

"What do you expect of me?" he shouted back. "You want me to just shut it off? You want me to simply ignore how I feel about you? How hungry I feel when I'm around you? Damn it, Lux. This is killing me."

For an unsure moment I cast my eyes to the floor, while my fingers played over my tender and bruised lips. "You were hurting me."

"I'm sorry." He gripped my arm and pulled me to him. "That's how badly I want you. I can't even measure it out in small, tender doses like I should. I just want you. I know you're fighting it, for whatever reason, but I think you want me too."

"All of that doesn't matter right now, Brax. We have to focus on getting you out of this curse. Don't you want that?"

"Yes."

"Well, then…?"

"Is this all because of Moore?"

Taken aback, I looked at him. "What?"

"Moore. You know, the other guy you've been spending a lot of time with."

I heard the bitterness in his voice and was torn between running from it or trying to diminish his anger.

"You know, the funny thing about that is that Moore has the very same problem I have. He has the same curse that I have, yet, you never really seemed too disturbed by that."

"You have no idea what disturbs me, Brax." Despite my desire to remain calm and keep my cool, I could feel the anger rising up my throat.

"Moore is just as incapable of controlling himself and his emotions as I am, yet…"

"Stop it, Brax."

"Why? Because you don't want to hear the truth about your own feelings."

"Moore works very hard to control himself and his power over me. He knows how dangerous it can be."

"Great. Now you're telling me that I should take lessons from Moore."

"Fine, if that's the way you want to be, I'm out of here." I turned and reached for the door, but he grabbed my hand and pulled me back.

"What, are you in a rush to head back to Moore? Is that what you've been doing lately? Spending all your free time with him?"

"The way you're talking to me now, Brax, you don't even deserve an answer, but I'll give you one anyway. I haven't see Moore for a few days and I have no idea what he's up to. I came here hoping to help a friend, hoping to help someone I care deeply about, but if you just want to go on about my friendship with Moore..." I tore my hand free of his hold. "You can get yourself out of this hell you're in."

I stormed out, angry and hurt. While my boots stomped the hardwood floors, my heart pounded with dread. I didn't really want to leave him. What would become of him?

His footsteps shook the floor, shook the walls as he came after me. "Lux," he said. "Wait."

Though I wanted to stop and hear him out, my feet continued to carry me away.

"Lux, please."

I heard his voice just over my shoulder and expected him to grab my hand again to stop me, but he didn't. He simply murmured my name... a plea.

"I didn't come here to fight with you, Brax." I managed to cease the advance of my feet, but couldn't quite bring myself to turn to him.

"I know."

"Do you think we could both calm down and just talk about this?" I glanced over my shoulder at him.

His fingers tentatively reached out to barely touch mine. "Please stay."

"Okay, but only if you promise to keep Moore out of this."

He grinned, boyish and adorable. "I promise."

"Look, why don't you go back and relax in the library, and I'll go fix us each a good strong cup of cappuccino. Maybe together we can find a way to jog your memory and get you back to when you entered the locker room."

"Sounds fair." He kissed my brow and affectionately pinched my cheek.

Smiling I turned to head to the kitchen. Braxton's uncle sure knew a thing about luxury. Though I'd been in the impressive mansion several times, I still marveled at the enormity of it. When I reached the huge and modern kitchen, I soon realized Brax should reconsider his decision to let go of the help. The kitchen was in dire need of a scrub down. A pile of dishes occupied a large portion of the counter and the sink contained pots and pans caked with dry food.

"Geez, Brax," I muttered as I picked up a dishcloth with the very tips of my fingers.

Footsteps sounded behind he and I turned to chastise him. "How can you let your uncle's place go like this, Brax?"

I turned to find an empty kitchen. "Brax?"

Silence.

With a shrug, I turned to find the espresso machine amidst the mess. I cleared the debris away and pulled the machine closer, then opened the cupboard to find the tin of coffee. As I opened the tin, however, it wasn't the aromatic scent of coffee that tinkled my nostrils, but the pungent and acrid scent of sulfur.

"Brax?" I called out as I spun around and pinned my back to the counter. "Brax!"

With trained eyes, I scanned the expanse of the kitchen. The scent was strong, as if it came from right under my nose, but I could see nothing out of the ordinary. I'd always had the ability to see demons and felt increasingly nervous as nothing came into view.

The air in the room chilled and the hair at the back of my neck spiked. I'd fought in the dark before; in fog, mist, in blinding light, but I'd always had the ability to see something. Now I felt vulnerable and naked... defenseless.

As though to prove my point I felt a heavy blow to my shoulder which sent me sprawling to the floor. Before I could get my bearings, the invisible entity grabbed me by the scruff of the neck and sent me flying across the kitchen where I slammed into the refrigerator door.

I scrambled to my feet and gazed blindly at the space in front of me. There wasn't even a hint, not even a ghostly image of a demon. Whoever this demon was, he was absolutely pure in his invisibility.

My heart pounded and I tried to control the knot of panic that slowly built up. This wasn't the time to lose my head. Visible or not, the demon had to be destroyed. Sulfur rose to my nostrils, so strong I almost gagged, both from the odor and from the knowledge he was close… too close.

"Lux," Brax shouted as he entered the kitchen. "Your crucifix. He's right on you."

I reached for the black cross hung around my neck just seconds before cold and callous claws clamped down over my throat.

Brax rushed to my side, took a hold of the invisible being in front of us and I reached out to touch my crucifix to it. Instantly the air changed. The scent dissipated and the temperature rose.

"You okay?" Brax pulled me into his arms and pressed his lips to my brow.

"How'd you know?"

"I smelled something funny and wondered what you were up to," he said with a wry grin. "I know you're not too handy in the kitchen so…"

"Cute. Seriously…"

"I did smell something," he said in a more serious tone. "And as I got closer the smell got worse. Pungent and stinky."

"But you saw him."

"Of course I saw him, but you didn't, did you?" He held me at arms length and looked at me, his eyes full of concern. "You were just staring blindly in front of you. You were looking right through it. What's going on?"

I pulled away and grabbed a stool to sit on. "I don't know." I was reluctant to share my fears with him. "I smelled him. At least there's that, but I didn't see him. I didn't see anything."

"I'm going to have to keep a closer eye on you."

I looked at him. "I didn't see anything in the locker room either," I confessed.

"Has this ever happened before?"

"Never. I don't understand."

"Maybe you should have a word with Moore about it."

"I thought we were past that," I snapped.

"I'm not trying to start this whole thing with Moore again. I'm serious."

"And why should I talk to Moore, then?"

"Well…" He hesitated and seemed embarrassed to go on. "I think he knows a lot… about them. He…" He pulled up another stool and sat beside me. "He came to see me after the whole Shayne thing."

"He did?"

"He wanted to apologize for what she'd done. He said he felt awful for the part she'd played in what happened to my parents and the curse I live with."

"I can't believe he did that. That's so sweet of him."

"Yeah," he muttered. "That's the reaction I was hoping for… he's sweet."

I immediately regretted praising Moore so openly, but I was truly proud of him. For him to be able to set aside his jealousy in order to personally apologize to Brax... it took a big man...

"Anyway, he sure seemed to know a lot about demons and being cursed. He told me quite a bit about what I was about to go through. Tell you the truth, I was mad at him at first. I was still in denial and didn't want to believe any of it. There was even a moment there where I wanted to smash his face in just for telling me about it all."

I cocked a brow, surprised by the ferocity of his words.

"But I've since come to appreciate what he told me. It helped me accept what's happening to me and it's given me a few tools to better deal with everything."

"Like what? I want to be able to help you however I can."

Before answering, he got up and went to the sink where he filled two goblets of water and came back. He handed me one of them and drank from the other. After a long series of gulps he looked at me. "In a way, it's all really simple. He said I should cling to the good things in my life, that I should hold that up as the goal, as the reason for fighting this. Every time I feel defeated and want to let go, I should think of all the things I hold dear... all the people I hold dear." His gaze softened as he looked at me. "I'm sure it's no surprise, but you're the reason I want to fight this so badly. I know I'll slip up from time to time, but I really do want to survive this."

"And I'll do everything to make sure you do survive this, Brax, for me and for everyone else who cares about you. But more than anything, you should consider doing this for you."

Chapter 3

Hunger

Moved by Moore's visit to Brax, I decided to pay him a visit of my own. I arrived at his impressive mansion with a chill of the few times I'd been there with Shayne. She was gone, led to hades by Braxton's parents and other demons, but I could still feel her presence, her sexuality and her desire permeating the entire mansion.

When Moore opened the door to let me in, it was clear her disappearance had left a void in the big, luxurious house.

"I haven't seen you for a few days," I said as I followed him to the back deck. "How're you coping?"

"Fine. Okay. Great." He sat back in a teak lounge chair spread out by the pool. Scratching his head, he gazed at me. "Okay, maybe not so great."

"That's what I was afraid of. Not seeing you these past days, not hearing a word from you, I had a feeling something was up." I pulled a deck chair up to his and sat facing him.

"It's getting worse," he confided. "Since the portal's been opened, I have trouble finding my true self within. It's sounds so ludicrous, but that's how it feels. I don't even know myself anymore. I do things I would never do. I say things I don't even think. The other day I took a box load of photos of Shayne when she was young and dumped them in the shredder."

"That's understandable, Moore. She put you through a lot."

He nodded somberly. "I walk around the house a lot and I've been in her room a few times. It still smells of her. A lot of her clothes is still lying around. I didn't touch anything and I gave strict orders to the help not to even step inside her room."

"I can imagine."

"Then there are days I can't go in there at all. I want to tear everything up. I want to rip everything apart. I want to punch the walls out. I'm so mad at her, but at the same time, I feel the effect of the portal that was opened. I can sense the intensity of the demons that were released. Dr. Kingsley did so much to hold them back, but they're coming and they're strong."

"I think we've already had a taste of that at St. James."

Moore looked at me and waited for me to explain.

"Asher chased a demon into the locker room. Not long after we found Bobby Fleishman's drained body in a shower stall."

"The lacrosse defense guy?"

"Yeah. Worst of all is that Brax was there."

"And what? You think he had something to do with it?"

"Not really, but he shoved Asher into a locker and doesn't even remember doing it. He doesn't remember being there at all. On the other hand, I was just at his place and I was attacked by a demon."

"You okay."

"Yeah, just barely. Funny thing is I couldn't see it, but Brax could." I pressed my lips together and shook my head. "I don't get it."

Moore nodded knowingly. "Actually, that proves my theory. The ones coming through at the moment are the strongest ones because the portal had just barely opened, and only the strongest ones can seep through at the moment, because the gates are still trying to resist their force."

I noticed the creases of concern on his forehead. "You worried?"

Nodding, he reached out to gently finger the back of my hand. "These stronger ones, the ones that are managing to get through, they're harder to fight, harder to resist." He swallowed and it was obvious he was pained by his struggle. "Fighting their influence has gotten virtually impossible."

"Don't say that, Moore. I know you're strong. I know you can resist this, no matter how strong they are."

"Believe me, I'm doing my best. It takes every ounce of energy, and there are days when I don't know how I'll manage, but…" He squeezed my hand. "I couldn't live with myself if the metamorphosis was to become complete. I couldn't live with the thought I'd harmed you in any way. And that's what's keeping me fighting."

The love in his eyes touched me and made me want to get closer to him. I could feel the warmth of his fingers over mine and immediately sought the unhealthy pull of the demons. But there was none, just peace and hope.

"That's what you do to me," he said.

I looked quizzically at him.

"The whirlwind and turmoil of this battle, of constantly fighting the demons in my life is calmed and soothed just by being with you."

Pleased that I meant so much to him and drawn to the sensual curve of his lips, I leaned in to kiss him. So dark, so mysterious, so dangerous... so delicious.

"I guess in a way, I'm soothed by you too." I brushed my hand over his cheek and sighed.

"I know a few more ways I could sooth you." He trailed his fingers over my forearm and up to my shoulder.

Despite the heated thrill that shot through me, I remained cool and sat back. "I think I'm good, thanks." As attracted as I was to him, I couldn't afford to let my emotions take over. None of us could.

I looked at him, trying to keep my gaze as detached as possible, but I knew hunger and desire flirted on my lips. I was good at controlling my emotions, but not that good. I wanted to soothe him and take away all the pain he was feeling. Moore had proven his love for me over and over again, and I wanted to do the same. I reached over and gently kissed him on the lips.

He nearly jumped when he realized I had kissed him. "What happened to the 'I'm good' part, Lux?" he asked, his lips curling into a seductively sweet smile.

I trailed my fingers over his arm and to his broad-shoulders and looked into his beautiful eyes. "I couldn't stand seeing how sad you were, Moore. I wanted you to feed off of me…whatever goodness and peace I have, I wanted you to feel it, too."

He sigh, his eyes roamed my face with such tenderness. "You're my angel, Lux," he said before leaning in to kiss me. "You're the one I've been waiting for all my life."

Chapter 4

Seeker

With a new dean assuming Dr. Kingsley's position at the university, I gathered Asher, Brax, and Moore together with the hopes of raiding Kingsley's office.

"This is cutting it close, don't you think?" Asher asked as we rounded the corner that led to the dean's office. "Didn't you say the new dean was already in?"

"Yeah," I said with a regrettable shrug. We'd concentrated far too much time searching for anything that could tell us how to stop the curse on Braxton and Moore in Dr. Kingsley's office at home, but had neglected to take a look at his university office. "But now we're here and we have to make the most of it. I have a visit to my dad as an excuse for being here and Brax is justified in wanting to pick up a few things left behind by his uncle. Between the two of us, we're covered."

"Then why'd you bring me along?" Asher grunted.

I patted his cheek. "We might come upon something we can't physically leave with. Maybe something in his office computer. If it's in Latin, I'm going to need you to translate for me."

"Will do."

Moore looked expectantly at me.

"You're my back up," I said.

"How's that?"

"Shayne was instrumental in raising money for the university. I'm sure this new dean is going to be just as hungry for funds. If ever he walks in on us and suspects anything, you're going to approach him with your fundraising ideas and a generous check."

"Why is it that I always end up playing the part of the pretty boy or the rich brat?"

Braxton glared at him, but said nothing.

"Okay, here we are. The new dean should still be at the alumni welcoming luncheon. Let's hope he's not paranoid and doesn't lock his door." I put my hand to the doorknob. It didn't give.

"Not to worry," Brax said. "I found my uncle's complete set of keys, including many of the offices here." Beaming, he held up one key. "Including the one to this office."

He slipped the key in and turned the knob. "There you go, milady."

I offered him an exaggerated curtsy and entered the realm of the dean of university. Wood, leather and the scent of sweet tobacco engulfed us as we entered the large, but surprisingly stuffy office. The heavy wood furnishings were overpowering and the thick drapes hung over the large windows barely letting in a ray of light.

"Did it always smell like this or is it just stuffy because it's been closed off for a while?"

"My uncle liked it dark. He found solace and security in the obscurity."

"Great, but it doesn't help us find his computer," Asher said with a smirk.

Brax pulled out every drawer of the desk and flipped through the sheets of paper he found in each. "Nothing," he said as he slammed the last drawer shut.

Asher scanned the bookshelves. "Nothing out of the ordinary here." He pulled one out. "School books," he said with disdain.

Then he spotted a large cigar box and let out a long, low whistle. "Cool cigar box."

"Yeah, my uncle liked a good smoke every once in a while, but that's not just a cigar box, it's a humidor."

"Well, let's just see what he kept in his humidor." He lifted the beautiful brass cover. "Paydirt, baby."

Inside the humidor was a sleek and shiny laptop.

"Great." I came to hover over his shoulder. "Think you can find something interesting in there?"

"I'll certainly do my best."

I gazed around at the young men with me. Moore stood at the door, ready to divert any attention away from us. Brax continued to look around, his eyes filled with chagrin and curiosity. He picked up a few items and set them in the duffle bag he'd brought.

"There's a password just to open the damn thing."

"Try Margaret."

We all turned to look as Brax.

"He once told me of a girl he loved when he was younger. He never really got over her and often thought of trying to contact her."

Asher punched in the name. "And voila. In we go."

"Nice screen saver," Moore called out from his watch at the door.

I glanced at the screen; glistening white mausoleums of a New Orleans cemetery against a clear blue sky. My eye was immediately drawn to an angel perched atop a tomb. Sad and praying, it looked up to the gods.

As Asher quickly typed away on the keyboard I saw pages open and close on the desktop. "So far this is all university mumbo jumbo. Nothing interesting; a speech he was to give; an invitation he meant to send out; notes for a meeting with the faculty."

"Keep looking." I gave him an encouraging pat on the shoulder and went to stand by Brax who seemed to grow grimmer by the minute. "You okay?"

"Yeah." He shot me a tight grin. "Just kind of weird being in here. At home at least I feel I have the right to be there, but here… It just feels like more of an invasion… an invasion of his privacy."

"You know we wouldn't be doing this if we didn't have to."

"I know, and I'm not blaming you for any of this." He looked over my shoulder at Asher and called out, "Just hurry it up so we can get out of here."

"I'm doing the best I can." His fingers continued to fly across the keyboard while a series of pages opened and closed. Finally, he saw something that interested him. "Hey, guys. Come look at this."

We gathered behind him and peered over his shoulder.

"What is that? His email account?" I asked.

"Yeah, but look at this contact." He pointed to a line. "Custos porta."

"What's it mean?" Moore asked.

"Custos is guard, or custodian. Porta is a gate or door; an entrance."

"Gatekeeper," I whispered.

Asher opened a few of the exchanges, and scanned the foreign and ancient words. "Look at this. This goes all the way to Venice."

"In Italy?" My heart pounded. Dr. Kingsley contacted people in Italy. Was it for personal reasons or for something more dire."

We all looked at each other, knowing what had to be do but not wanting to say it aloud.

"I think we're going to have to leave with this baby," Asher said.

"For all we know it was Kingsley's personal possession. The new dean should have no need for it."

"Fine," Braxton said. "Take it. Let's just get out of here."

"I'll make arrangements to have my jet ready." Moore opened the door. "We should be good to go in an hour or so."

We all nodded.

Chapter 5

Flight

"What are you looking up?" I sat beside Brax and glanced at his open laptop.

We were four hours into our flight to Italy and everyone had been quiet, caught up in their own thoughts, plans or fears.

Three laptops were open; Moore's served to find places to stay while in Venice; Asher continued to search every file in Dr. Kingsley's documents and Brax had just opened his.

"I thought I'd take a look to see what I can find out about this secret society my uncle frequented."

I pulled the Book of Angels onto my lap and flipped to a few key pages. "I've been trying to find out more about the society in this book."

"Since when do you read Latin?"

"Asher's been helping me. He gave me a few key words to look for. Hopefully I'll find something useful before we arrive; either about the society or about me."

"And hopefully I'll find out more precisely where we need to go."

Each with our own research, the jet became silent save for the sound of the engines and the titter tatter of laptop keyboards.

"I think we may need to change trajectory," Brax said after another hour.

"Now?" Moore complained. "We're almost there."

"I'm finding more and more activity in Rome, not Venice."

"Ditto," Asher said. "I just found a file with dozens of exchanges between Dr. Kingsley and a Delphino... in Rome. The Vatican to be more precise."

"Great," we all muttered in unison.

Something ominous and dark weighed down on all of us. The Vatican; the big league.

"I'm not too surprised," Moore said. "Now that I think of it, Dr. Kingsley once mentioned a trip to Rome. It was a while back. Shayne had prepared a charity auction and he'd told us he couldn't attend because of this trip. He'd made nothing of it and had simply told us it was a matter of a few speeches and a bit of tourism at the same time." He nodded and stood. "I'll go give the pilot the change in plans."

After a few minutes I went up to the front of the plane to make sure everything was okay.

"Hey," Moore said when he spotted me. "What brings you up here?"

"Just wanted to make sure this last minute change of plans was okay."

Moore shrugged. "It's a bit of a hassle, but no big deal, but now that I have you alone…"

He pulled me into his private room on the jet and silently closed the door behind us. "I've been wanting to do this all day." His hold of me tightened and he leaned in to kiss me. There was little tenderness in the embrace that was possessive and urgent. "These past days, it's been hard. I miss you, even more than I would have thought possible. I have a lot on my mind, what with Shayne, the portal and everything, but you… you're at the forefront of my thoughts… all the time."

I didn't want to admit aloud just how I'd missed him. More than anything I wanted his heated kiss to continue and to evolve into something more. I wanted to lock the door and spend the next few hours cuddled up to him, kissing him, touching him and getting closer and closer.

"I think I've already told you just how much I love you, how much I want to be with you. You don't say much in return, but I have a pretty good idea how you feel about me as well."

He paused as though giving me a chance to deny or confirm his statement. I simply grinned and laid a soft kiss on his lips.

"If we feel so strongly for one another, why can't we just come out and make it official, exclusive? Why can't we announce that we're a couple?"

"Moore," I said in a tone that was more plaintive than I'd intended. "This isn't really the time to start up this conversation again."

"Right." He tightened his hold and edged me back to the foot of his bed. "Why waste time on a conversation about being a couple when we can simply be."

With the back of my calf against the bed, I put a strong hand to Moore's chest and stopped him from nudging me onto the bed. "I think we should get back to the guys."

"Why?" His eyes were heavily hooded and his grin took on an aroused curve.

"Seriously, Moore."

Shoving his tongue into his cheek with a petulant groan, he released me and backed away. "You're still hung up on what I am, aren't you?"

I pressed my lips tightly together and blinked quickly in an attempt to contain the sudden spring of tears. "It's not something I can easily ignore, Moore."

Though no tears flowed, I could feel their weight on my lower lashes, and by the look in Moore's eyes, Moore had noticed.

"Do you love me, Lux?" He cupped my cheek while his thumb plied the flesh just under my eyes, releasing a few tears. "Really love me?"

Nodding and casting my gaze to his belly I said, "I can't."

"But you do," he whispered.

"To love you could mean the end of me, Moore."

"To cease loving me could be the end for me." He scrunched down so that his eyes were level with mine.

I couldn't help but smile, however meekly, at his determination.

"In addition to loving you, I need you. I need your support. I need to know you're on my side as I try to fight the darkness that's overtaking me. God help me, Lux, but it's getting strong and stronger. I always thought of myself as a strong guy... fearless, but this..."

"We'll stop it, Moore. I have no doubt we'll find answers to many of our questions in Italy. The Vatican, Moore. It doesn't get any bigger than that. If they don't have the answers..."

"Yeah..."

Fear of not finding the answers was evident in his eyes. This big, strong and fearless young man now eyed me with boyish uncertainty. More than anything I wanted to soothe his fears and tell him everything would be okay, but truth was, I couldn't be certain of that. None of us could. The Vatican could bring answers and solutions, just as it could bring more questions and problems.

The only course of action I found for the time being was to assuage his fears with a tender kiss. "I'm not going to give up on you, Moore. No matter what happens, I'm not giving up." My hunger and passion for him took over and I enveloped his lips with mine, hungering to taste him, to transmit to him the emotions I couldn't speak aloud.

He kissed me back with a ferocity that left my head spinning. Finally he pulled back and smiled.

"We should rest before we arrive," he said. "All of us."

"I'll go back and tell the guys we should be in Rome in an hour or so."

"No," he said. "I'm sure they can come to that conclusion on their own. Let's lie down and try to sleep."

I glanced at him with doubt and suspicion.

"No joke." He held his hands up in a protest of innocence. "I promise I won't lay a hand on you. We really need to rest."

"Hmm… I've heard that one before."

Despite my protest, I laid down beside him and before long was deep in sleep.

Chapter 6

Race Against Time

The plane touched ground at Fiumicino Airport, just outside Rome.

"I found us a few hotel rooms just outside the Vatican city," Moore explained as we all stepped off the plane and into a waiting rental car.

"I was able to find a more precise address," Brax said as he took the front passenger seat.

Moore quickly punched the address into the GPS and sped off, leaving Asher and I just barely enough time to get our seatbelts buckled. The car swerved around a corner, skidded through a curve and sped like a bullet down the straight away.

"Hey," Asher called. "You think you could just get us all there in one piece?"

Unamused, Moore glanced in the rearview mirror and glared at Asher. Saying nothing, he swung onto an onramp and once on the highway, gunned it.

Asher smirked and looked at me with a shrug. His sparkling blue eyes were filled with humor despite his protests. "Guess we'll just have to pray we make it in one piece."

Smiling, I said, "I'm sure he knows what he's doing."

Our eyes remained locked and I could have sworn he felt the same worry and concern for Moore that I did. Either the concern was that evident in my gaze, or he had come to be so in tune to me, so in tune to my emotions, that he was able to easily reflect them.

"Hey," Asher called in an uncharacteristically cheery voice. "I think I'm having a serious case of déjà vu."

"You've been here before?" I asked.

He stared out the window, looking at the beautiful buildings and scenery. "I don't think anything's changed. I think I came here, what, nine, ten years ago."

"Good to know if ever we get in a bind," Brax said, though his tone lacked enthusiasm or conviction.

"Yeah," Asher went on. "My parents were on tour here and we went to the Vatican. I was barely seven years old, but I distinctly remember being on this very highway. Think we could stop to get a bite to eat before we take care of business? I'd love to go and get a few shots of the Vatican while we're there too." He pulled a small digital camera out of his jacket pocket and took a few quick snaps of me.

"I know we're here for serious business," I said, getting into the mood Asher tried to create. "But I really think I'm going to enjoy this trip. I've always wanted to visit Rome. Do you think we'll have time to take in the Coliseum after the Vatican?"

"I'm just looking forward to seeing the Sistine Chapel," Asher said.

"And St. Peter's Square," I added.

The cheer Asher and I tried to bring to the tension riddled car ride did little to dent the stress and strain evident in Moore and Braxton's eyes. So much was riding on this trip and their eyes told the full story of their fears.

Worse still; the palpable tension that filled the small car wasn't just human. An incubi aura, strong and consuming, hung close to Moore and a faint incubi aura was beginning to shimmer around Brax.

Asher and I fell silent, and though I refused to let the somber mood take over me, I realized there was nothing Asher or I could do to alleviate the fear Moore and Braxton lived with. All we could do was be there to help get them through it.

Chapter 7

Chosen Path

As it turned out, the Vatican wasn't our first stop. Without giving us any indication as to where we were really going, Moore took to the highway and headed south. Silence reigned as we drove through the Italian countryside. No comments were made about the rustic homes, the green pastures or the roaming and grazing animals. Even when we came upon a small group of young Italian women walking on the edge of the road, the guys remained unmoved and unimpressed.

We passed through small towns and villages, some with small modest homes, others with impressive and welcoming villas. The further we went, the more I felt tension fill up the car. No doubt the guys were all looking forward to getting out of the car and finding some good Italian food. The flight had been long and fatigue was also beginning to play on everyone's nerves. We'd have to find a restaurant and a place to sit back and relax soon.

That moment came a long hour later when Moore finally pulled the car into the narrow lane of a small and tightly built village. Each building seemed to ooze history and mystery. As we filed out of the car, I also realized many of these buildings oozed fabulous scents and appetizing aromas.

"Where's the food?" Asher asked, cheerily. "I could go for anything right now."

"I don't think we'll have any trouble finding something suitable." Moore took the lead, and no one argued his position.

"This is beautiful; so rustic," I exclaimed as we found a larger boulevard.

Void of crowds and tourists in this little village, we had free reign to meander through the streets easily and carefree.

"It is nice," Brax said, though a little half-heartedly. "Where are we, exactly?"

"Velletri."

"Vel-let-tri. Vel-let-tri," I chanted. "Sounds so romantic. What does it mean?"

"Loosely translated, it means city by the swamp," Moore said. "But it's a city rich in history and I think we may be able to get a few answers to our questions."

"Well, it certainly looks romantic," I said, unperturbed by the origin of the name.

"And smells like heaven," Asher said. "When do we eat?"

Moore stopped, turned to put the tips of his fingers to Asher's chest and said, "Hang out here a minute. I'm going to go check in here to see if we can't get a bite to eat."

He disappeared for a few minutes and returned with two hot cappuccinos. "Here you go." He handed me a cup. "There's pizza and stuff if you guys want to go in and eat."

Asher sprinted for the door, and though Braxton dragged his feet behind him, he went in all the same.

The moment they disappeared inside the small ristorante, I turned to Moore. "You okay?"

"What gave it away?" He grimaced and gazed around in annoyance.

"You've been agitated since we got here, and you're practically turning green. What's going on?"

"I don't know." He shook his head then took a forced sip of his coffee. "Food just doesn't appeal to me right now."

"Could be just your nerves playing with your appetite," I ventured, though I knew full well it went much further than that.

"I can't get the thought of draining someone out of my head."

Though I'd expected this kind of thing, I was nonetheless shocked by his confession.

"It's becoming an obsession. I can barely think of anything else. I can barely see straight."

"Despite all that, you're doing a great job of controlling yourself. Just being able to drive us here. That took a lot of concentration, Moore." I wanted to give him something to cling to, something to be positive about.

He sighed and avoided my gaze. "It's getting harder."

"I know," I said with a reassuring pat to his shoulder. "How about we try to find a way to get you to think of something else?"

"Like what?"

"Like showing me around."

He gazed sidelong at me.

"Come on." I gave him a friendly nudge in the ribs. "I want to have a bit of fun before we get down to the business of getting to these demons and the portal."

Swallowing, he gazed down at the paving stones beneath his feet. Without looking at me, he reached for my hand and gave it a quick squeeze.

"Come on." I tugged on his hand and urged him on.

After another half-hearted sip of his coffee, he set the cup down, forced a grin and led me down a narrow street. I stopped to look in shops, touching fabrics, smelling spices and admiring local art. Moore remained lackluster in his enthusiasm, but he dutifully guided me from shop to shop and even led me to the Porta napoletana a beautiful arch that marked the northern gate of Velletri.

"Have you ever been here before," I asked. He seemed so knowledgeable and took to the streets as though he'd always traveled them.

"No," he said. "I've never even heard of this town before."

I wanted to question him, but sensed his growing irritation. He led me through the streets with a sense of direction and never once looked up to check a street sign or ask for directions. It was odd, but I didn't want to argue.

When we came to an old little chapel, I took the lead and guided him to a bench facing a small but lovely fountain. I threw a few pennies into the fountain and smiled. "Hey, would you mind taking a few pictures of me?" He looked at me, his eyes dark, his mouth grim and his overall posture defeated.

"I don't think I can beat this, Lux. I'm sorry. I really wanted to show you around and show you a good time, but…"

"I don't want you to feel the pressure of pleasing me, Moore. I just thought it'd be a nice distraction." I looked around. Though we weren't in the optimal peak tourist season, many people walked around, mostly locals going to work, going to lunch or running errands. "Come with me."

I led him to a quiet, out of the way lane. "You're an incubi and the tension will only get worse. I want to do what I can to alleviate all the pressure you have pushing down on you." Cupping his cheeks I pulled him to me and kissed him with all the passion I had. At first he pulled back, hesitant and unsure.

Though his lips clearly hungered for mine, he pulled away. "Lux, what are you doing?"

"I don't want to see you hurting anyone. I want to do what I can to relieve the pressure."

His gaze dulled, and I could see the fear he had for me. "I don't want to hurt you, Lux," he said softly.

"I don't think you will. I don't feel the incubi pull as much from you anymore. I think it may be because I have angel blood in me and you've managed to try to block off any of that with me. You've been doing it for so long, you don't even think about it. Not like Brax, who has a harder time with this. I want to help you," I whispered. "If you need to drain anyone, or kiss anyone, let it be me. Last time you were having a hard time with this, when we kissed, it seemed to calm you down. And if you do start draining my life out of me, I have my crucifix ready."

He looked at me, his expression changing from fear to love in a matter of seconds. "I can't let you take this risk, Lux."

"I want to," I said. "If this is a way to help, then we've may find the way to break this curse permanently. You don't have to worry about hurting me ever again." My fingers trailed up to his temple and back through his thick hair. Pressing my lips to his I murmured my desire for him, encouraged him to let go and lured him into my passionate embrace.

My hands roamed over his body, reveling in the sensations his strong build brought to my fingertips. It didn't take long for him to release the last of his inhibitions. After only a few seconds, he grabbed me and pulled me to his chest.

Our embrace and kisses hit a fever pitch as we grappled to get closer still, tugging at each other's clothing, longing to have skin on skin contact.

"It's incredibly... what you do to me. I can barely hold back," I whispered as my lips still brushed against his, my eyes locked to his.

"Are you afraid it's just the incubi in me that attracts you?"

I'd thought of that possibility, but was happy he'd been the one to bring it up. But now that the question was out there, I didn't know what the answer was.

"Or is it simply because you're truly in love with me?"

I chuckled softly and leaned my brow to his lips. I'd also thought of that possibility. Yes, the physical longing was there, and the incubi in him probably had something to do with that, but I also felt a deeper connection to him; a connection that had nothing to do with how physically drawn to him I was.

"I guess we'll just have to rid you of this incubi to find out."

He planted another passionate, but softer kiss to my lips. "I can't believe how lucky I got when you came into my life. I need you, Lux. Not just to help me with this curse, but I need you in my life. What did I do to deserve you?"

A ferocious growl thundered through the walls of the chapel, cutting our romantic interlude short.

"Did you hear that?"

Moore nodded.

"I was hoping we'd have more free time, but I guess the fight is about to start."

Moore nodded.

We rushed to the front door of the chapel. The doors were locked and we hurried to the side entrance reserved for priests. Inside we stood amidst hundreds of lit candles, everyone of them casting eerie shadows on the walls and ceiling.

Through the shadows we spotted a couple on the front pew. A young woman, her skirt up to her hips straddled a young man who sat back, his chest bare and gleaming with sweat and soot. Lost in their embrace they were oblivious to our presence.

"Could we have confused their innocent moans and groans for a feral growl?"

Moore cocked a brow as the young woman arched her back, offering a generous view of her breasts. "Doesn't really look all that innocent to me," he said with a smirk.

We stood for a moment, unsure as to what our next move should be, but before we could make a decision to interfere or leave the young lustful couple alone, a dark and fast moving shadow sprang out of nowhere and descended on the couple.

In a flash of movement, the dark shadow pulled the woman off the young man and threw her against the wall. She stumbled and tried to straighten up to fight off her assailant, but the shadow was far too quick.

I caught the shine of gold as a small crucifix was pulled from the shadow and pressed to the young woman's brow. Her explosive demise was as spectacular as it was surprising. In a spray of blood, flesh and ash, she faded to nothing.

Moore and I gazed at each other, perplexed by the goings-on of the small church. A part of me wanted to rush the shadow and stop it from hurting again, but another part of me questioned the true identity of the young and wanton woman.

Unaware of our presence, the shadow remained still a long moment, and seemed to recover from the interaction with the young woman.

Moore's elbow nudged me in the ribs and I turned to find him gazing at the young man. Following his gaze I saw the shell of the human being he'd once been. All that remained was a shriveled body that sat back on the pew in an awkward pose of death.

"What's going on?" I whispered.

The drained body lost its hold of the pew and slid to the floor, catching the attention of the dark and somber shadow who slowly approached it. A sad and mournful chant came from the figure as he passed his hand from brow to belly and from shoulder to shoulder.

He turned his gaze toward the heavens, but halted.

We'd been spotted.

Chapter 8

Inheritance of a Legacy

He took one step toward us, then another. My fingers flexed and clenched while the beating of my heart took on that of a seasoned warrior. It was hard to tell if he was good or bad, angelic or demonic, but I wasn't going to take any chances. Of average height and build, he offered no true threat, but I also know of smaller, less intimidating demons who showed unusual ferocity when backed to a corner.

At my side, Moore tensed up just as much as I did. I could feel his readiness.

Another step and my fingers instinctively reached for the crucifix at my neck. There was something unfortunate and unpleasant about battling in a house of worship, but these types of battles didn't always wait for the most favorable opportunity.

"Show yourself before taking another step," I warned. To make my intentions clear, I held my crucifix up to him.

The dark shadow turned to the glow of candles and pulled back the black hood that obscured his face, revealing the handsome but troubled face of a white-haired man.

"You are a demon hunter, are you not?" the man asked with a heavy British accent. His eyes remained on my crucifix.

I nodded and jutted my chin up to him. "And you?"

He appeared to be in the same age bracket as Dr. Kingsley, though perhaps a little younger. Despite the shock of white hair, he had brilliant blue eyes that sparked with youthfulness.

"Yes," he said simply. His eyes narrowed as he glanced at Moore with suspicion.

Could he see Moore's true nature; the curse he lived with? Would he be tempted to slay him before he showed any potential threat? I wanted to jump forward, to explain, to defend and to justify, anything to stop this man from hurting Moore.

Unperturbed, Moore stood his ground, staring the older man down and showing no fear.

"What are you doing here?" He adjusted the cloak around his shoulders and seemed offended by our presence. "Are you Americans?"

"We're from San Francisco." Moore's voice boomed and echoed around the small chapel.

The man's brow rose with interest, but he said nothing.

"We came here to find someone, or perhaps a group of people," I said. "Through a series of emails received in America, we found the name Shadow Light and we were hoping to find him."

He nodded and his gaze remained steady, giving nothing away. "And your search led you all the way to Italy? Why are you so eager to find this shadowlight?"

I heard the low and impatient growl that harbored in Moore's throat. The incubi in him was surely working him up, and standing face to face with a new and strange demon slayer no doubt added to his strain.

Taking a determined step forward, Moore stood barely a foot away from the man. "A portal's been torn open and we think this Shadow Light might know how to shut it down."

Hoping to shut him up before he went on, I stepped forward and put my hand to his arm, but he pulled away and went on.

"You say you're a demon slayer. Then you should know something about portals and the way demons go through them to get into this world."

"And what makes you think I would know about such a thing." He glanced at me, his teeth clenched in annoyance. "You have a professed demon slayer right there with you. Doesn't she know the workings of the portal?"

I could see we would lose this man's cooperation completely if Moore continued to intimidate him. "Sir, I apologize for my friend's harsh ways," I said as I stepped forward. "Moore has been through a lot lately and this portal opening is testing his patience at every opportunity. I may be a demon slayer, but I've never had to deal with a portal opening, at least not one of this proportion."

His gaze remained hard and uncompromising. Moore took another menacing step toward him, but this time I took a firm grip of his arm and pulled him back.

Standing between Moore and the British demon slayer, I tried to take the role of mediator.

"Please, not only do I not have the ability to close this portal, I'm also losing my ability to see demons at all. In certain instances I can still smell them, but I otherwise have no sense of their presence. This new influence, this new influx of demons since this portal opening is getting stronger and stronger, and the change is happening fast."

"We also know that Dr. Kingsley had several communications with Shadow Light," Moore interjected.

"Perhaps the answers you seek reside in this Dr. Kingsley. Your hop across the pond may have been in vain."

"Unfortunately, Dr. Kingsley is no longer with us," I said. "And his death has left the burden of mending this open portal to his nephew, Braxton. We've come here with him in the hopes of helping him."

The man's expression changed dramatically at the mention of Dr. Kingsley's death. "Did you say his death?"

Feeling a shift in his emotions and deducing he'd known Dr. Kingsley, I nodded solemnly. "He was killed by a demon. It truly devastated everyone. In addition to the loss of someone we all loved and cared about, we also have a batch of stronger demons to contend with. Please," I said as I reached out to him. "Is there anything you can do to help us?"

He turned away, troubled by the news I'd given him. For a long moment he faced the large crucifix behind the altar. "Kingsley has a nephew," he finally said in a small remote voice.

Frowning I gazed at Moore and he nodded. "Yes," I said.

"And he is now the gatekeeper?"

"Yes."

Turning to face us, he shoved each hand in the other's sleeve. "Is he here? In Italy?"

Unsure of this man's motives, I hesitated.

"If he's been designated the next gatekeeper, it's imperative I know about it. You must take me to him and we have to move fast."

Still reluctant, I gazed at Moore for guidance.

"Please," the man said. It was his turn to reach out for me. "We really have to act quickly."

"I don't want to offend you, sir, but I can't take the chance of putting Braxton in harm's way. Tell me what you know about the secret society Dr. Kingsley was a part of. Tell me who this Shadow Light is."

His grip tightened on my wrist, but not with aggression or anger, but with urgency and need. "I will tell you everything, but please, let me find this nephew of Kingsley's."

Guarded and tense, I turned to Moore who nodded. Seeing his clenched fists, I knew he was ready for any eventuality.

"You better take the lead, Moore. I wasn't really paying attention when you brought me here."

The older man shot me a curious glance, but made no comment. We followed Moore out and wove through the narrow streets. Every street corner seemed to look like the last and before long I was completely disoriented.

"We've known this was urgent from the beginning, but why does this have you so worried?" asked the man as I tried to recognize the streets we passed.

The older man looked at me as he pulled his hood over his head. "As the powers transfer, so do the responsibilities. With Kingsley gone, a replacement much quickly be put in place. Kingsley was raising this nephew, was he not?"

"Yes, Braxton lived with his uncle until his death. I believe they spent a lot of time together and Dr. Kingsley tried to take a place in Brax's life after the loss of his parents."

"We just have to hope that he's been grooming him for this. Hopefully Kingsley considered what would happen if ever he died."

"I'm not really sure whether he did or not."

I suddenly wanted to find Braxton and fast. "Are you sure we're headed the right way?" I asked Moore. With every step I felt the sense of urgency grow.

Before Moore could answer me, the small eatery we'd left Asher and Brax in came into view.

"Hey, where'd you guys run off to?" Asher said as he dropped the remnants of his pizza crust onto his plate. "We wanted to wait for you before eating, but you guys never showed. We saved you some pizza, but it might be a bit cold and…"

His voice trailed off and his eyes met with those of the hooded man who'd followed us in. "Who's your new friend?"

Brax looked up, his eyes searching for recognition as he looked into the blue eyes of the man. He took another bite of his pizza, but it was clear his attention was entirely on the man in the cloak and not on his food. "I know you," he finally said.

The older man poked his hand out from under his cloak and held it out to Brax. "And you must be Kingsley's nephew. I do believe I see a small family resemblance."

Brax remained oddly cold and indifferent. "You came to visit my uncle once. You two spent hours in his study, talking."

Nodding, the man let out a dark chuckle. He pulled back the chair beside Braxton and sat down, his eyes pleased as he looked at the nephew he'd seen before.

"Who are you?" Brax said.

"Yeah," Asher shot in with a defensive tone. "Who are you?"

Moore and I stood, watching and waiting.

Suddenly unhurried and relaxed, the man pulled a slice of pizza from the large plate set in the center of the table and took a big hungry bite. He chewed, slowly, languidly, as if he had all the time in the world. "Never waste perfectly good pizza," he said.

Watching him take another bite, I was suddenly famished. The scent of spicy tomato sauce came to my nostrils and I sat down to take a large piece.

Pleased, this strange man who'd been so rushed moments earlier, looked at me with a grin. "Bloody good pizza." He held up his slice to show me then glanced up at Moore who still stood, waiting. "Pull up a chair and have pizza."

"You made me race across town to get you to Brax," he argued. "And now you want me to sit back and eat some damned pizza."

"Moore, please. Give him a chance." I reached up to grasp his fingers and soothe him.

"Who are you and what do you want with Brax... with us?"

"Please," the man said. "Sit down. I will tell you everything."

Chapter 9

Time to Mend

He finally introduced himself as Markus, though he offered little more in the way of information. The pizza seemed to please him immensely, as though he'd not eaten in days, and while he questioned us on our trip to Italy, our appreciation of our surroundings and the people we'd met so far, he didn't delve too deeply in our backgrounds, angelic, demonic, or otherwise.

There was no talk of the events Moore and I had witnessed at the small chapel, and he almost gave the appearance of a plain and rather ordinary man, hooded cloak aside.

I bit back a hundred and one questions, and I could see the guys were anxious to see the conversation elevate to something more profound, but Markus seemed intent on keeping the discussion light.

"Okay," he said after an eternal amount of chewing on his last bite. He clapped his hands free of any remaining flour and crumbs, in no way rushed to finish his thought. "I think I may have something of interest to show you chaps. What sort of transportation have you been relying on since your arrival?"

"We have a rental," Moore said with some impatience and bitterness. "A small rental."

"Think you can squeeze me in?"

We left the small eatery and soon found out.

As it turned out, it was a tight squeeze, but we all managed to get into the car. Markus took the front passenger seat and, with more finesse and just as much accuracy as any GPS, he guided us out of Velletri and onto the country roads of Italy.

Markus offered various comments on the expansive villas we passed and told us a bit about the history of the province of Latina, through which we drove. But for all his chatter, there was nothing profound or pertinent... it was all interesting, but trivial.

Scrunched up between Braxton and Asher in the back seat, I gazed from one to the other as Markus continued his idle chatter. Asher shrugged his shoulders, which cause a bit of a domino effect across the seat, and Brax simply stared at Markus as though preparing for an attack.

His face solemn, he reached for my hand and squeezed my fingers. Though we lacked the liberty to speak aloud our doubts and suspicions, I could feel Braxton's fear in his very fingertips. He was unsure of this hooded man, this Markus who led us to undisclosed destinations.

I concentrated my gaze on the sceneries we passed, not so much in an attempt to enjoy the ride, but more to remember the roads we'd taken and the twists and turns. Somehow I need to grasp something concrete, like where we were exactly and where we were going. I couldn't help but feel disturbed by the ignorance Markus kept us in and being able to itemize the various views gave me a bit of reassurance and a sense of security, however false that sense of security might be.

The makings of a small town began to creep through the picturesque countryside and soon we were driving through cramped streets and up to an imposing monastery.

"Impressive, is it not?" Markus said as he stepped out of the car and stretched his limbs.

We all looked at the building that was indeed impressive.

"The beauty of gothic straight from twelfth century," he went on as he led us to the double arched gate. "The architecture was meant to be somewhat sedate, almost austere, all the better to pray without distraction."

For all its austerity, there remained something opulent about the building.

In the distance we could hear the faint echoes of chants, dark and mysterious in their melodies; haunting in their harmonies.

My breath was immediately taken away as we entered the church. Two wide aisles led to the chancel, accented with streamlined pilasters. The enormous vaulted ceiling, so high above us, was painted with various biblical scenes.

Though the scenes depicted were angelic, uplifting and celestial, I felt the tension that passed from me to

Moore, to Brax, to Asher and back to me with added intensity.

Thankfully, a few people sat in the front pews, their heads bowed in prayer. I found a degree of comfort in knowing we weren't alone.

Markus took on a reverent stance as he walked down the aisle. He led us out to the cloister then opened a small and uninviting door. A dark and narrow stairwell greeted us and the tension I'd felt from the guys moments earlier was multiplied tenfold.

The chants could be heard louder now, bringing parishioners to great heights of prayer, and no doubt bringing solace and enjoyment to the young monks who milled about with various chores. But the chants seemed to bring only an added weight to our ever growing uncertainty.

Each step we set our foot to was cracked, chipped and uneven, making our descent into the darkened belly of the monastery a tedious undertaking. I had to steady myself on the cold and clammy walls. As we reached the last step, the ceiling seemed to fall down over us, making everyone have to stoop in order to avoid smashing their heads.

In sharp contrast to the high ceiling, celestial images and heavenly light of the church above, the under belly had a ceiling that left Asher and Moore in a perpetual hunch. After a few meandering corridors, we emerged into a large den that was both surprising in its beauty and disturbing in its richness.

Ornately carved bookshelves lined one wall while a large and majestic oak table took up the center of the large room. The ceiling rose, coming to spike in the center, right above the table. At the table sat two men, both intent on the computer screen before them. They appeared to be in the same age bracket as Markus, but were dressed more in the fashion of Dr. Kingsley as opposed to that of Markus.

At first sight they gave the impression of being academics, rather than priest demon slayers, like Markus. My curiosity was piqued as I tried to connect the dots. What did these men have in common with one another and what did they all have to do with us? It was hard to imagine these two finely dressed men involved in anything demonic. It was impossible to think they could possibly hold the key to ridding Brax and Moore of their curse.

The smaller, more delicate of the two stood and looked directly at me. After a moment of scrutiny, he removed his glasses and gazed briefly at Brax, Moore and Asher before bringing his gaze back to me. Without his glasses and with the hint of a tense smile on his lips, he appeared a little younger than I'd originally thought. Still very handsome, he had a tight, square jaw that made him look serious and subdued, but with eyes that blazed with mischief and a touch of danger.

Beside him, the broader and slightly more portly man remained seated, almost unaware of our arrival. There was something a bit European about him, though I couldn't quite put my finger on what country. There was something almost Grecian in his profile, but he had startlingly blond hair.

Though he'd surely been very handsome when younger and thinner, there was something intriguing and attractive about him. He exuded confidence, almost arrogance. Perhaps it was in the way he barely gazed our way, or in the slight smirk that came to his lips when he did.

"Who among you is called Braxton?" the dark haired man asked.

For a tense and silent moment, no one responded. Then Braxton stepped forward. "I'm Braxton Kingsley."

"Good. Good. And I'm Gordon Green." He gazed down at his silent partner and arched a tense brow as he tilted his head toward us.

As he stood, the fair-haired man seemed intent on avoiding my gaze. I swallowed the sudden sense of self consciousness that came over me. I'd often felt uncomfortable under intense scrutiny and detested having anyone stare boldly at me, but something in the way he avoided me... it touched an odd chord inside.

"My name is John," he said. His full height was impressive and I could now see that he wasn't portly, but built like a bulldozer. His arms were thick and muscular, even through the tight button up shirt. His massive chest stretched the shirt taunt.

"I sent an email to one of you," Brax said. "Which one of you is Shadowlight?"

Markus went to stand beside John and Gordon. "We are," they said in unison.

Brax glanced back at us, a frown of frustration and confusion on his brow. "What?" he said as he turned back to the threesome. Shadowlight isn't just one person?"

"No," Markus said. "It's all of us. We form Shadow Light, along with your uncle, Dr. Kingsley."

Shadow Light: Beautiful Beings Book 3

"And what, exactly, is Shadow Light?" I asked as I stepped forward. We'd wasted enough time and I was anxious to get to the point. For the past few hours we'd heard nothing but the idle ramblings of an older Englishman and I now wanted answers; real answers.

Gordon and John exchanged annoyed glances then looked at Asher and me.

"If anyone should know, it would be the two of you," Gordon said.

"So I assume it has something to do with angels, then," Asher said.

Gordon nodded. "Yes. Shadow Light is the light and energy source of angels. The light takes away the shadows. Or, if you prefer, it's an allegory for demon slayers blessed by sight and aided by angels who take away the darkness... the shadows."

I glanced at Asher and could see he'd never heard of such a thing. Turning back to the men, I said, "So, does that mean that you're demon slayers and not angel?"

"That's right," Gordon said. He clasped his hands in front of him, giving him a more academic look than he'd already had.

"And can you help us find what we need to do to close the gates that have been opened in San Francisco?"

Gordon looked to John and Markus before answering. "Yes."

"And what about the curse that's been put on Moore and Braxton?"

"There are as many curses as there are lost souls. It depends on the nature of the curse. Do you know what curse it is that they live with?"

"They're both turning into demons. It was a slow transformation at first, but since the portal's been opened, the change has been coming surprisingly fast. That's why we came out to find you guys. Do you think you can help them?"

All three men looked at each other, as though a silence conference was quickly being held between them. Eyes narrowed, lips tensed and all three gave a barely perceptible nod. Without more warning than that, Markus and Gordon charged Brax, while John turned his attention to Moore. All brandished their crucifixes and for a frightening moment, I froze.

"Hey," Asher shouted, springing me into action.

I hurried to step between John and Moore, while Asher quickly moved in to block Gordon and Markus from Braxton.

"What are you guys doing?" I blurted out. "I thought you said you could help rid them of the curse."

"We can," John said, his crucifix still held up and ready to slay. "By slaying them."

"Are you crazy?" I shouted. "That's not what we came here for." Maintaining my fighting stance, I turned my angry gaze to Markus. "I thought you were bringing us here to help us, not slay my friends."

Chapter 10

Drop of Truth

The determination in their eyes was intimidating. Despite my years of experience, despite the hundreds of situations I'd been in over the years and the thousands of demons I'd slain, I felt small and out of my league before these demon-slaying men of age and wisdom.

How long had these guys been at it? How many slain demons did they have under their belts? How easy had it become to slay a demon?

Gordon finally softened his gaze somewhat and took a step toward me.

I wasn't fooled by this gentler approach and remained on guard.

"The last thing we want to do is hurt you, Lux."

The hairs at the back of my neck instantly rose at the sound of my name on his lips. Though I might have mentioned it to Markus as we'd sat down to pizza, I knew beyond the shadow of a doubt that it had not been told to Gordon.

"We really don't want to hurt you at all," John added. For the first time, his gaze remained steadily on me. As harsh as he'd been since our arrival, his eyes softened and even he looked concerned and moved. For a moment of hesitation, he turned a quizzical gaze to Gordon then faced me with a warm smile. "I can hardly believe how you've grown into such a beautiful and smart young woman."

The foreboding chill that'd spiked the hairs at my back now sent off a series of alarms throughout my body. There was more going on here than the mere attempt to slay Moore and Brax. This was more than a simple attempt to close the portal.

"I'm so pleased with how you turned out, Lux."

"Somehow I doubt you've earned the right to call me Lux in such a familiar way, and you certainly have no right to show any pride in the way I've grown up."

"I beg to differ," he said. "And I'm sure Ida would agree with me."

His riddles were playing with my nerves. "Ida?" I grunted with open irritation.

He came to face me and reached out to grasp my shoulders, but I quickly back away. There was something increasingly disturbing in the familiar way he'd suddenly taken with me. As cold and remote as he'd been earlier, he now showed too much interest in me.

"I'm sorry," he said. "But I neglected to introduce myself properly. My name is John."

"Yeah," I snapped. "So you said."

"John Collins."

My breath choked me and darkness closed in, leaving me with barely a narrow tunnel of vision. I didn't want to hear more. I didn't want to know. My mind flew back across the Atlantic, across the United States and I was back in San Francisco, back in my parents' house. I didn't even want to hear the connection I could have with this man. Could this man who was going to slay two of the friends, my loves even, be related to me?

"Yes, Lux, we share the same family name, and I know that's shocking to you. I hadn't really expected that we would meet like this, under these unfortunate circumstances. It's funny how you look forward to an event in your life, yet when it comes it leaves you breathless; maybe a little unsure."

I frowned. Was he the one left breathless by our encounter, or should I be?

"To you, this encounter is the first, but I've known you for ages, Lux. I've known you all your life, if only from a distance. And though it's been quite a while, I would have recognized you anywhere. There's an aura, a spirit that surrounds you that's unmistakable."

"Could we get past this lopsided reunion and just get to the gist of it? Who are you and how do you know me?"

"Lux, I'm your father."

I laughed; laughed so hard it startled every man in the room. My laughter, an odd sound that bordered on hysteria, echoed throughout the room and through the maze of corridors. "Right," I finally muttered breathlessly. "My father."

My gaze, maniacal as it felt, circled the men around me. "And who are you?" I asked Gordon. "My long lost brother." I nodded at Markus. "Some estranged uncle?"

"Lux," John said in a tone meant to soothe. "I know this is a bit difficult to take in, but…"

"Difficult to take in?" I said. I wanted to hurl something at him; something heavy, something blunt. "I think you've been watching too many movies, Mr. John Collins… too many George Lucas movies. How 'bout we get back to reality?"

"What he says is true," Gordon said.

"I don't really care what you say." I set my hands defiantly to my hips. "I don't believe you."

"Lux," John said. "If you don't believe me, let me prove it. I know you have a slight cleft on your ear; your right ear."

My hand automatically reached for my right ear.

"The cleft is the result of your birth. You were a big and strong baby. Ida, she's a relatively small woman. But you were determined to push through and, before the doctor could set you right, your ear dented in the birth canal."

I stared dumbly at him, my fingers working over the little indentation at the top of my ear.

"Considering the difficult birth Ida anticipated, things turned out pretty good. After all, a little dent on the ear is nothing."

The rush of blood to my cheeks left me hot and weak. I wanted to sit down, but didn't want to give them the satisfaction of having beaten me down. I wanted to be strong. I wanted to be unfazed by his declaration.

Glancing at Moore, Asher and Brax I saw the shock I felt reflected in their eyes. This wasn't exactly the revelation we'd come all the way to Italy to hear.

"Is it true, Lux?" Asher said. "Do you have a cleft? Is he your father?"

"I am," John said before I could answer.

"If what you say is true, how did I end up with my parents?

"Under the circumstances, Ida and I thought it'd be safer for you, for everyone. I can't say it was an easy decision to come to, but my brother, the man you've come to know as your father, had a stable life and a healthy relationship. Ida and I spent hours talking about it, hours trying to find the best solution and this is what we came up with."

Shaking my head, I thought of my mother and father. They'd always been so loving. Never had they even given any indication I wasn't completely and utterly theirs.

"I knew they would give you the safe and loving home you deserved."

After a long hard and desperate moment of staring at him, he offered more. "As a demon slayer, my life gets dangerous. I find myself constantly in perilous situations. Surely you have an idea what I'm talking about."

I nodded.

"As a gatekeeper those perilous situations are amplified, and with Ida a demon slayer as well, your safety would have constantly been compromised."

"So you're saying that the people I've come to know as my mother and father are actually my aunt and uncle."

"Technically... biologically yes, but I'm sure they would always want to be thought of as your parents."

"Yes," I said, feeling a tinge of guilt. "Of course. I'll always think of them as my parents. They raised me and were always there for me. Even when I began to show signs of the demon slayer I was, they..."

I looked at him, saddened by this new knowledge. "Even when things got rough, all the suspensions from school, all the times we had to move all the changes that had to constantly be made... they never gave up on me. They could have easily turned their backs on me. They could have called you... and this Ida... asked you to come back and get your troublesome child."

John smiled. "From what I've heard over the years every ounce of trouble you might have caused them was far outweighed by all the joy you brought to their lives. They couldn't have children of their own. You were a blessing to them and from the very first moment we put you into your mother's arms, they've loved you as though you were theirs."

"You are a gatekeeper," I said. Though I still didn't understand it all, my tone softened.

"Yes," he said. "And I have been for over thirty years."

"Does that mean that I'm to be a gatekeeper one day? Am I to take your place the way Brax is to take that of Dr. Kingsley?"

"Ultimately, yes."

"So you should have been training me, preparing me for gatekeeper duties," I challenged.

"Hmmm, well... I..." He stammered and stumbled, then looked sheepishly at me. "I was planning on eventually finding you."

"Eventually," I echoed with sarcasm. "Did you forget where your brother lived?"

Pressing his lips together, he glanced at his cohorts.

"I'll admit I may have been a little negligent. Demon slayers don't often have holidays. We didn't have too many chances to get away."

"You could have had me sent here?"

"You have the answers to everything," he shot back with an amused grin. "I like that. Not only did you become a beautiful young woman, but you've got a head on your shoulders."

"Okay, regardless of your reasons and excuses, Brax needs to know what to do to close the portal... now. The gate was opened in San Francisco, and with that, thousands of demons have been coming through. To make matters worse, I'm losing my abilities. I have trouble seeing them and fighting them is getting impossible. And Moore is..."

"A demon, Lux," John said. "Who would eventually bring you down if you don't slay him now. Cut all ties, which we were trying to do for you so you can avoid doing it yourself one day," Gordon said.

As though the sound of his name broke him from a trance, Moore lost whatever remnants of control he had. With surprising force and uncharacteristic fury, he charged Gordon. The surprise attack left Gordon on the floor and Moore then turned his attention to John.

Just within inches from grabbing John by the throat, Moore was jumped and subdued by Gordon and Markus. They each had their crucifix ready to slay.

"Asher, quick." I shouted.

"I'm already on it." Before I could reach them, Asher had gripped both Markus and Gordon's wrists and twisted them away from Moore.

"This doesn't bode well," John said with a regrettable shake of his head. "This doesn't bode well at all."

"What do you expect from us?" I shouted. "We came here for your help and all you've given us is the threat of being slain and some ridiculous story about my history."

"Lux," John said. "I know I'm not your father in the true sense, but I have to tell you… You shouldn't be in the company of such a man as Moore. No good can come of it."

"You're right," I said. "You're not my father in the true sense, therefore you have no right to tell me who I should and shouldn't spend my time with."

"As a demon slayer I believe I have not only the right, but the responsibility to tell you. The demon in him is winning and it's just a matter of time before he strikes out at you."

"That's not going to happen. Should Moore ever become that uncontrollable, I'll be ready." I could barely look at Moore as I said that, trying to appear calm in front of the Shadow Light demon slayers. I knew in my heart as much as I try to fight it, the day I have to slay Moore would be the day I give up demon slaying.

During my mixed emotions and confrontation with John, I was vaguely aware of Asher's movement as he walked away with Gordon. My eyes barely registered he had left the room with Gordon. For what, I wouldn't know.

John was looking at me and I could have sworn there was pride in his eyes. "All right. Fine. We'll do things your way. There's really nothing I can do about it for now, so I guess I'll just have to trust that you'll know what to do when the time comes… and that you'll have the strength to go through with it."

While I helped Moore up, I looked at John. "I'll do whatever's right." Although Moore was smart enough not to say anything at the moment, I felt him stiffen beside me, and I wanted to reach over to hold his hands, but stopped. If I showed any emotions toward Moore right now, John would have slain him. He seemed like the type who would not tolerate second chances and was quick to nip anything in the bud before it went further. Although he claimed he was my father, I still kept a distance from him, ready to defend Moore and Brax with my life.

A few moments later Asher rushed back into the room. "Okay. I have it."

"Have what?" I asked.

Moore and Brax looked expectantly at him.

"I just learned how to close the portal. This in turn should subdue the demonic urges you guys feel." He looked pointedly at Moore and Brax.

For the first time since arriving in Italy, I felt a real ray of hope. I'd begun to think there was no way of getting

Moore or Brax out of their predicament. I turned to shoot a victorious grin at John and Markus, but stopped when I caught the chagrin in their eyes.

The ray of hope dimmed somewhat as I anticipated the price we were going to have to pay.

Chapter 11

Abundance of Destined Plans

Additional chairs were brought around the large table. Heavy, cumbersome and ancient, they were far from welcoming.

"Please," Markus said as he brought a chair up behind me. "Let us all take a seat, take a breath and take a moment. We need to talk this all out."

I glanced at Moore, knowing the suggestion would bode well with him. I couldn't really blame him. On two occasions they'd charged him and it was easy to imagine they'd do it again.

"You guys really think we want to sit down and talk... to you?" Moore glared at our hosts with murder in his eyes then turned to Braxton. "You want to sit and talk to these clowns?"

"Moore," I said, hoping to calm his anger. This wasn't the time to lose his cool.

When he turned to look at me, I didn't recognize the hard, menacing eyes that stared at me. "Are you hoping they'll do what you're incapable of? What you've been wanting to do all along? From the very first moment you met me, you've wanted to slay me."

Stunned by his glare and the accusation, I fell into the chair Markus had so strategically set for me. "What are you talking about, Moore? I'm the one who stopped them from slaying you."

His stare remained hard a long moment before finally softening. "Yeah," he muttered in a tone on the verge of defeat and desperation. He was confused and getting worse.

I turned to Gordon and John then glanced back at Markus who still stood behind my chair. "We have to do something fast. They're taking over him. He's losing all control. Soon he'll be lost to us completely."

John's gaze on Moore threatened to explode, but he made no move to attack Moore again.

"If we could all be seated," Markus said. He gestured for Moore to take the seat at the other end of the table. "Maybe you'll feel better if you put a bit of space between us."

With a brooding grunt, Moore pulled back the chair, letting the legs scratch loudly across the stone floor. When he sat down I breathed a quiet sigh of relief. Everyone took their seats.

"I had a nice chat with Asher," Gordon said after a tense moment of silence. "I'll admit I didn't hold much hope for the situation you all find yourselves in when I first set eyes on you. Asher is like no other guardian, angel, or demon slayer I've ever known."

"Well, if you're hanging out with a bunch of old cronies," Moore droned. "It can be a bit surprising to find yourself in the company of younger men."

John and Gordon exchanged glances, but didn't comment on Moore's outburst

"What our fine gentleman is trying to say," Asher threw in, "is that he severely underestimated my capabilities. It's not the first time people have looked at me and thought I was just a useless kid."

The anger he felt for his parents' constant absence glistened in his eyes.

Gordon grinned tightly and gave Asher his best attempt at a paternal pat on the back. "But I've come to realize that he is, indeed, a fine young man with a good soul. A good young man who can do so much."

"You don't need to sell us how good a person Asher is. We know," I said with a touch of testiness. Annoyed by the slow pace of the conversation, I wanted to push him to get to some answers.

"I understand, but I thought it worthwhile to share with you just how I've come to appreciate what lies beneath the hard exterior of this rough-looking young man. I've met plenty of demon slayers over the years, but I've rarely met a young man with the strength and wisdom he shows."

"All right. All right. Stop it already," Braxton said in a hollow tone. "His head is big enough as it is. Can we move on to other things?"

"I was surprised to learn," Gordon went on. "That Asher had a Book of Angels, and even more impressed when I learned he'd almost read it through. As you may or may not know, all gatekeepers have a Book of Angels."

"Why?" I asked. Somehow, I'd assumed the Book of Angels we'd found at Dr. Kingsley was the only one of its kind.

"Despite our years of experience, we still need help from time to time. The Book of Angels gives us guidance in moments of uncertainty. It gives us instructions in times of confusion." He set a large Book of Angels on the table.

It looked older than the one we had and slightly thicker.

"These books have been passed on through the ages. No one is really sure just how old they are, or from where they came. All we know is that they give us the answers we need."

"My uncle never showed any signs of being a demon slayer. Why is it that I never noticed anything?"

"That's because he wasn't a demon slayer. He never was. Your uncle was strictly a gatekeeper. The academic you knew was who he truly was, but he was never a demon slayer. Many gatekeepers aren't, but this can sometimes put them in dangerous predicaments. As a man of refinement, your uncle frequently found himself in need of help; urgent help. Gatekeeping is never pretty. That's where men like us came in. A demon slayer was always assigned to guard over him, to protect him... that is until something happened to him."

"What do you mean?" Brax asked.

"Demon slayers are often killed. It's not an easy life and we lose one from time to time. Others are simply re-assigned; sent to work in another area, for another gatekeeper."

His words echoed in my ears as I stared at him. In just a few seconds he'd explained so many things I'd never understood; he answered so many questions that seemed to have no answer. Something had happened to the demon slayer assigned to cover Dr. Kingsley, and it had left the dean of university unprotected and vulnerable.

Surely he knew. He had to have known he was vulnerable. He'd said nothing... after all, who could he tell? But he had the power to bring me close, and he used that power. I no longer had any doubt Dr. Kingsley had put everything into place so that I could go to St. James Academy. He'd arranged for my family to move to San Francisco to begin with, and he ensured I was close by giving me access to a school I never would have been admitted to under normal circumstances.

It also explained my instant attraction to Brax. From that very first moment, our eyes had connected with a purpose, and I finally knew what that purpose was.

I glanced at Brax and remembered that very first time our eyes had met. New to San Francisco, I'd felt lost and alone. Sitting in the back of my parents' car, it was easy to feel frustrated at having to start all over again at a new school, with new faculty, new students, new problems.

But I'd seen him, even though the car spent less than three seconds in front of Dr. Kingsley's lavish home, I'd seen him, and in those three seconds, I'd connected; I'd known.

"We were supposed to meet," I said to Gordon, though my eyes remained on Brax.

"Dr. Kingsley didn't always keep us abreast of all the goings-on in San Francisco," John said. "He was a very independent man who liked to deal with situations on his own whenever he could. It saddens me greatly to hear that we've lost him."

"With what you've told us, we conclude that he knew he was open for an attack. So, yes," Gordon went on. "He probably made the arrangements that would bring you two together. Whatever he lacked in fighting skills, he made up for in foresight."

"I wish I'd known," Markus said. "It would have been a pleasure for me to go to America to help the good doctor, but I've just recently acquired my gatekeeper status. A relative of mine went on to other things, and I took up for him."

"That's why he didn't recognize you when you found him in the chapel," Gordon explained.

"Then why didn't either of you come to help Dr. Kingsley?" I said to Gordon and John.

Shaking his head with regret, Gordon glanced at John before answering. "Scheduling demon slayers isn't as easy as it appears. We work everywhere, though we're more often found in the eastern hemisphere. Africa, Asia and mostly Europe."

"We were supposed to see him seven months ago," John said. "We try to all meet up at least a few times a year. We catch up on what's going wrong and what's going right, but he was a no show at the last meeting. He didn't travel much and coming out to Europe wasn't really something that tickled his fancy much."

I looked to Brax. He'd mentioned a trip his uncle had taken to Italy. Why hadn't he met with these gatekeepers?"

"Maybe he knew it was already too late and he preferred staying close at hand," I suggested, while my mind sought other answers.

They shrugged. "Maybe."

"So this all leads to me becoming a gatekeeper?" I said.

Gordon nodded. "We believe that just may be the case, but there's something more. It's easy to see there's something more to you... something special about you."

John beamed as his eyes caught mine. "I always felt Ida's family had been touched by an angel. Her brother often had an aura around him and her younger sister carried something divine in her. Ida herself never showed any angelic signs, but she apparently managed to pass the valuable genes on to you all the same."

"In addition to becoming a gatekeeper, you think I may have angelic powers as well." It was all a little too much, and this new information just seemed to bring about a whole new batch of questions.

The jet lag, lack of sleep and anxiety ridden day was finally catching up on me. I felt exhausted by it all, but was reluctant to mention it. There was so much to do. My brain was in a fog and I wanted a moment to put everything aside. Then again, I wanted to ensure I gave it all plenty of time to sink in

"If I'm so blessed with these angelic powers, if this Ida you keep speaking of gave me her angelic genes, why is it that, after years of finding and fighting demons with barely any effort at all, I now find myself almost blind to them. I can't see them anymore."

"At all?" John said with a touch of concern.

"I was attacked recently and I never saw him. He was right in front of me, inches from my nose and I never, ever saw him. So what's going on?

Chapter 12

Portals

"Portals have been found in numerous areas of the world. While many were predictable and foreseen, others were a complete surprise." John led us to a portal he'd been guarding for months.

As we strolled through the Italian countryside, it was hard to believe a portal to Hades existed in such a beautiful setting. When he turned down a dirt lane that cut through a vineyard, I couldn't help but be transported by the beauty of the area. Hills rolled away on either side of us and flowers bloomed in every direction. The home at the end of the lane was as grand as any home I'd seen in San Francisco, but with a flavor and style all its own.

"I love it here," I whispered to Asher. "Isn't there something so…"

"Romantic."

"And quaint and charming and… I don't know, relaxed, slow, unhurried. It's as if stress doesn't exist here at all."

"Well, with all this wine, I can see why."

The vines on either side of us were heavy with purple grapes that beckoned to be stomped.

"Do you think we'll be able to extend our stay?" I asked him, hoping for a break from the darkness that so constantly filled our lives.

"Are you bailing out on us?"

I smiled and looked at him. "There've been times in my life when I'd wished I could just chuck all this demon slaying aside and live my life like any other girl. This, right now, right here, happens to be one of them."

John led us to the back of the Tuscany style villa and walked up to a ground well.

"This, my friends, is Porta del Valpolicella." John looked at us with a grin. "We like to give them names that will help us associate them with their locations."

"How long has it been here?" Moore asked. He ran his fingers along the edge of the heavy stones that lined the portal.

"Perhaps you shouldn't get so close, Moore," I said.

He looked at me, accusing at first, then with a softened gaze of understanding.

"It is well guarded, I assure you," John said. "Though it never hurts to be cautious."

"So how is it that you guard this? You've been away from here and running around with us all day. Couldn't it have slipped open during your absence?" Brax looked at John with skepticism.

"Guarding a portal isn't a matter of perpetually standing at the gate. It is a matter of maintaining order, and I'll show you how that order is maintained." John pulled a small glass vial from his coat pocket. "Holy Water."

"I should have known," Asher said under his breath. "Holy Water… it's the answer to everything."

John glared at him and went on. "The maintenance of a closed portal is much easier than the closing of one that has already been allowed to open." He pulled out the cork of his vial and sprinkled several droplets along the perimeter of the ground well just beneath the stones. The moistened soil rippled and waved a few seconds before stopping. "Only a few drops are needed every day."

"That's it?" Moore grumbled. "You sprinkle a few drops of water and your work is done?"

"Not quite," John said, his eyes narrowed in annoyance. "There are a series of prayers and blessings that must accompany each benediction."

"Like what?" I asked.

John took on a solemn expression and raised his hands to the heavens. "By the powers of up above, and with the greatness of thee my Lord, I bless this area and ask for divine protection against the forces of darkness." The spots of soil that'd been moistened with Holy Water bubbled up, steamed and smoked. "Let your power reign on all that is good and let it prevail over evil." Once the prayer was over, the soil quickly cooled and returned to its normal appearance.

"Sounds simple enough," Asher said with a shrug.

"There are a series of these prayers and blessings to memorize and they must be said in proper order."

"How many do we have to memorize?" I asked.

"Seventeen."

"I practically have a photographic memory," Brax said. "Jot them all down and we're done here."

"Not so fast, my good man," John said with a sound clap on Brax's back. "There is also the matter of the tone in which you speak these words. You must convey conviction and belief. To utter them with bland indifference will get you nowhere."

John held up the Book of Angels he'd brought with him. "This book is indispensable. If you cannot memorize it, learn as much of it as you can and keep it close to you." He flipped through the pages and stopped to read a few lines. "Veritas diaboli manet in aeternum. Libera te tutemet ex inferis. Ad maiorem Dei gloriam"

"What is he saying?" I leaned closer to Asher and asked.

"I don't know. He's saying them too fast. I'm able to read and decipher a good amount of Latin, but I've never really heard it spoken aloud much."

With his finger still poised over his last spoken words, John looked at us all. "It is a simple enough task if your conviction is strong. A few moments of your day, every day, and the deed is done."

"But we believe the portal we're dealing with is already open."

"That will be a greater task, but the overall process is the same; more Holy Water, more prayers, more conviction. If the four of you band together, and work as one, you'll have a greater chance of success."

We looked at each other, realizing just how much we'd have to depend on one another if this was to work. Moore and Brax gazed at each other with heavy scrutiny and they both looked at Asher with doubt.

"That won't do," John chastised. "That won't do at all. You must trust one another, rely on one another and stay strong together. Don't forget that."

Chapter 13

Respite

As I woke up the next morning, my nostrils were assailed with the scent of wild flowers, steaming coffee and baked treats. It was a splendid morning and I wanted a moment to stroll my surroundings before everyone rose.

We'd found several small rooms to rent at a house nearby and had planned on spending another day with Gordon, John and Markus. We had spent a few days with the Shadow Light slayers learning as much as we could about portals and demon slaying. These men held so many years of experience, there was still so much to learn, but time was ticking by, and we did not have the luxury to of leisure. I don't know if it was the immensity of the task that awaited us at home that had them stalling, or if it was a true desire to learn as much as they could, but I sensed a reluctance to leave Italy in everyone, especially me.

Kailin Gow

Outside the scent of wild flowers was accompanied by the song of birds early in their hunt for their first meal. A small wrought iron table was surrounded by four delicate chairs and set atop the table was a bright blue ceramic coffee pot with four brightly colored mugs.

Reveling in the peaceful moment, I poured myself a cup of coffee and savored it. My body and soul filled with pure contentment.

"When was the last time you relaxed and enjoyed the moment like this?"

His voice was ragged with sleep, but I recognized Moore's deep and sensual voice.

"I don't want to sound melodramatic in saying never, but… never."

"A pity."

"I'm becoming painfully aware of that."

"We could extend our stay."

"If the situation in San Francisco wasn't so urgent, I'd agree, but…"

He came up behind me and wrapped his arms around my waist. "I could wake up to this every morning," he said.

"One day," I idly promised. Perhaps a life of leisure and luxury simply weren't in my cards. I was destined to fight to keep the world peaceful and free of demons. "My turn will come one day."

"Care to stroll through the gardens with me?"

I glanced over my shoulder at him and was shocked to see him standing there with only his jeans on. My eyes immediately narrowed with desire and strolling the garden was the last thing I wanted to do, but I turned around in his arms and smiled. "I'd love to."

He turned and slipped into a blue t-shirt then and took my hands. Modest, but filled with fragrance and color, the garden was a veritable Eden. Tightly packed with a variety of flowers, not an inch of soil was allowed to go to weeds or grass and little went towards a pathway. Moore and I could just barely walk side by side.

All the more reason to walk snuggled up in his arm.

"What do you plan on telling your parents?" he asked after a moment's silence.

"I have no idea." Not that I hadn't thought about it. It was a question that had haunted me since learning of John's relation to me. "I don't want them to think I accuse them of any wrong doing, or that I resent the situation.

They've done so much for me and I've been lucky to have them. Though I do have to admit I wish they would have told me themselves."

"I'm sure they would have preferred that as well."

I nodded and stopped at a brightly colored bird feeder. Several small yellow birds weaved in and out, picking up a seed and flying off to eat it in the comfort of their tree branch.

"Perhaps John will come with us to San Francisco and save you the trouble of having to find the words to tell your parents you know about them."

"Do you really think he'd come?"

"I asked him last night and he said he'd consider it."

"But the portal? He said he had to be there every day to maintain its closure."

"He said Gordon could take on the task if need be. I think he really would like to come."

We heard footsteps behind us and turned to see John coming down the path, a red mug of coffee in his hands.

"I thought I heard my name."

"I think it's best we leave Italy today," Moore said

"Certainly. Gordon is already sitting with Asher, going over the many Latin blessings and prayers he needs to learn. By early afternoon you should be free to go."

"And you?" I asked. "Will you be free to come with us?"

"I think it's a journey I've put off long enough. Just think of the surprise on my brother's face when he sees me walk through the door."

Though I was still nervous about that eventuality, I couldn't help but grin. Dad sure would be surprised, not to mention Mom.

Chapter 14

The Fifth Shadow Light Slayer

The flight back to San Francisco was a blend of tension, apprehension and anticipation. I barely had time to consider what would happen with the portal since all my thoughts were concentrated on how my parents would react to seeing John.

I dreaded the devastation my mother would feel and could only hope she didn't take it too harshly.

Gazing at John who sat across the aisle with Brax, I also felt a wave of reassurance. Having such an experienced demon slayer with us would be an added bonus and would lighten our load.

When the plane touched ground in California, we all got into our separate cars and cab, and headed home. The car ride with John was long and silent, and I wondered if he was as nervous about seeing his brother as I was about their meeting.

"Here we are," I said as the cab pulled up to my house.

"Not bad," John said as he looked at our home with an approving nod.

I stepped out and grabbed my suitcase while John paid the fare and pulled out his small travel bag.

"Should I go ahead and knock, or should you...?" he asked.

"I think it's best if I open the door and announce that I've brought a surprise... kind of to warn them that something is up."

My legs shook as I walked up to the front porch. I couldn't remember ever being so nervous, not even in the worst of the battles I'd been involved in.

"Mom," I called out as I opened the door, hoping they'd be home. "Dad?"

"We're back here, honey," Dad called from the veranda out back.

"I brought a surprise back from Italy," I announced.

"Really."

I heard a shuffling of movement as I rounded the corner and saw my dad heading toward us. The moment his eyes caught John, his face and entire demeanor changed. He stiffened and clenched his fists. His gaze darted back and forth between us; pain and fear as he looked at me, then anger and resentment as he turned to John.

"What's going on?" Mom said as she came to join us. Her face went chalk white as she saw John.

"What are you doing here?" Dad finally asked.

"I got word that I was needed and came."

My mother looked at me, her eyes filled with questions.

"Yes, Mom. I know. John told me all about it."

"Honey, I… I'm so…"

I rushed to her and pulled her into my arms, wanting nothing more than to erase the look of sadness and pain from her eyes. "Don't worry about it, Mom. I'm fine with it. Really I am."

"But…"

"How could you do this?" Dad asked of John. "How could you so blatantly put your nose where it didn't belong?"

"She's the one who came to me," John said in defense.

"For help, perhaps, but I strongly doubt she asked about your paternity."

"She is my daughter and if I desire to tell her…"

"You haven't been a father to her in years," Mom accused. "You've never been a father to her."

John gazed at me and shrugged. "Perhaps this wasn't such a good idea after all."

"Dad," I said. "You're right, he didn't have to tell me, but now I know and I'm happy I know. It makes me appreciate all the more the wonderful parents you've been to me. And, Mom, you're right, he's never been a father to me and he's not going to start now. I brought him over strictly to help with a matter at school. That's all."

Silence fell over the room as we all looked at each other.

"I know there's no excuse for my absence all these years, but I've never stopped thinking of her," John said. "And I have missed you, little brother."

Dad offered the first vague sign of a grin. "I guess that's what happens when you have a higher calling."

"I was just about to put on a pot of tea," Mom said. "Would you like some?"

"That would be great."

The ice had been broken and the awkward moment had passed. Dad beamed with boyish enthusiasm and Mom took on the role of the perfect host. While Dad and John headed to the veranda out back, I joined Mom in the kitchen to help with the tea.

She seemed distance and lost in her own thoughts while she filled the teapot. Saying nothing, I opened the pantry door and pulled out a few bags of tea.

"We often thought of telling you," she finally said.

Still silent, I pulled three cups from the cupboard and drop a tea bag in each.

"When you were young we argued that you were too young. As you got older it just felt wrong. We were doing so well together. Our family unit was strong and... I guess we were ultimately afraid of what you'd think, how you'd react."

"I can't hide the fact that it was a shock to hear that John was my biological father. Actually I was kind of upset at first and I didn't understand why neither of you had ever told me, but...."

As the water heated up, she crossed her arms and turned to me. "This is a scene we've always dreaded. I guess somewhere in the back of our minds was the possibility that John could just show up and show interest in you. As you got older, became an adult, we constantly anticipated his arrival."

"I guess you never thought I'd go out and bump into him."

"No, that we did not consider."

"Look, I'm not angry, Mom. Really I'm not. Whatever anger I might have felt at first learning about John has passed. I accept it. Please believe that and don't let yourself get upset. I've been told so many times that I have the greatest parents. Everyone envies me and I know I couldn't have asked for better parents."

The water announced its shrill arrival to the boiling point and Mom poured water into each of the three cups.

"Are you going to join us?"

I hesitated. This was a family reunion that still left me a little uncomfortable. Then again, I felt I had so much to learn, whether it is about John my father or John the demon slayer and gatekeeper. "I guess sitting with you guys for a little while can't hurt."

We joined the men who immediately stopped talking the moment we arrived.

"Do we have that big an effect on you guys?" Mom said with a dry chuckle.

"Actually we were talking about Ida." John reached for his cup of tea and sat back in the large white wicker chair usually reserved for my mother.

"Oh," Mom said with a quirky tilt of her head.

"You know, the moment I saw Lux, I knew who she was." He turned to look at me. "You guys did a great job with her. I'm just sorry Ida wasn't able to come with us; wasn't able to see her for herself."

"Well, maybe some other time."

Though Mom was being as diplomatic and polite as she could, it was clear she felt threatened by this Ida person.

"Ida has always been one of the most fearless demons slayers I'd ever known. She went into battles few men dared to. She faced ferocious demons that would have made many cry for their mommy."

Mom sat beside Dad while I took a seat beside the large potted plant in the opposite corner. There was something strange about talking shop talk in front of my

- 149 -

parents. Though they knew about my demon slaying abilities, it was still something I rarely talked about. If anything, the older I got, the more I kept my battles and fights to myself. Part of me didn't want to burden them with the troubles and the fear I sometimes lived with. Part of me just wanted to keep that part of my life private.

"I would have thought Ida would give up her demon slaying duties when Lux was born."

"It's not like a position in a national corporation that you can just resign and get a nifty little pension," John said with much sarcasm. "Demon slaying is…"

"Yeah, yeah," Mom said with an irritated wave of her hand. "I know, it's a higher calling. Spare me the rhetoric."

"Honey, what's gotten into you?" Dad asked.

"It's okay," John said. "I can understand her frustration. Her maternal instincts have just kicked in and she's feeling possessive about Lux."

"My maternal instincts didn't just 'kick in,'" she snapped. "They kicked in the moment you put Lux in my arms, and they've never wavered."

I'd never seen her so upset and it broke my heart to see her so troubled.

"Of course not. I apologize for my gauche manner with words. I guess what I really wanted to point out was your momma bear instincts."

The damage was done. Mom sat back and glared at John over her tea cup.

"As I was saying, Ida has always been a brave fighter, but she finally met her match a few months ago."

"I'm so sorry to hear that, John," Dad said. "What happened? Is she all right?"

"She was lucky to survive and many wondered how she managed. The blood loss was great and the first to find her assumed she was dead. A hearty soul found a pulse and had her brought to a hospital. She has been in a coma for months now. She barely responds to our voices or any stimuli."

"Perhaps it's a blessing in disguise," Mom offered, her tone now softened.

John looked at her with a frown. "How do you figure?"

"You say she was fearless and confronted any demon, no matter how ferocious or big. Well, perhaps a larger battle lay ahead; one that would really have finished her off."

"I'll be sure to transmit to her your positive outlook on the situation." John smirked. "Yes, at least she's alive."

Tension filled the room. Mom looked deep into her tea cup while Dad inspected the tiny cactus growing beside him. I gazed from one troubled adult to the other.

"What are the chances something like that ends up happening to Lux?" Mom finally asked. Tears glistened in her eyes.

While I'd thought the tension had grown from my relationship to John, I now saw it really had nothing to do with that. Mom was worried about me and by the look of concern in my dad's eyes, so was he.

"I'm not that fearless, Mom, so don't worry," I said, though somewhere deep inside I knew it wasn't completely true. I thought of the many battles I'd fought, battles I should have backed down from; demons I should have backed away from. Perhaps meeting the fate Ida had met was just a matter of time, but I wasn't about to let Mom have another worry on her mind. "I've never fought a demon I wasn't sure I could slay. And now even more than ever. I have Brax, Moore and Asher on my side. If I'm ever faced with a demon I can't handle, I have them to turn to."

"I'm sorry, dear," Mom said. "I didn't mean to make it sound like I didn't trust you. I know you're a smart girl and you have excellent judgment."

I got up. "I don't mean to cut this short, but I have some serious jetlag and I just want to get to bed." I kissed Mom dutifully on the forehead and winked at Dad. "I'll see you later, John."

Sighing as I walked out and headed to the stairs, I felt the weight of the world on my shoulders, and the fatigue that accompanied it. On top of everything I had to deal with, I now had the concern of my parents to consider... more than ever.

I'd barely closed the door to my room when I heard footsteps coming up the stairs. They were too heavy to be my mother's and too quick to be my Dad's.

"John," I said as I opened the door and let him in. "What can I do for you?"

"I know you want to get some sleep, but I just wanted a chance to tell you that I'm there for you. You mentioned how Brax, Moore and Asher are on your team. I'd like to think I'm part of that team as well."

"I guess that could work."

"There's also something else I'd like you to consider. I heard you mention you intermittent troubles with your vision. You see demons well, then you don't see them at all. You're losing your senses."

"Yes, it's been happening on and off for a few days now."

"I don't want to be the bearer of bad news, but this might indicate a need to put some distance between you and those boys."

"Those boys? What are you talking about?" I could feel the anger rising to my face.

"Moore and Brax."

"Why? Because you don't like them, because they're cursed?"

"Yes, Lux. Don't you see? Your inability to see demons is due to the time you're spending with Brax and Moore."

"I don't see what one has to do with the other. Are you just trying to find a way to make me stop seeing them?"

He shook his head. "You're becoming accustomed so the presence of demons and it's causing you to lose the ability to sense them. Think about what happens when you walk into a room where cookies are being made. The smell instantly assails your nostrils and you can immediately detect the scent. But if you remain in that room for an extended amount of time, the scent seems to diminish and you don't notice the smell of cookies. So much so that when someone else enters the room and notes on the smell of cookies, you still don't smell it."

I looked at him, wanting to criticize his theory, but it made too much sense, and I hated him for it. "I'd never really thought of it that way."

"I can imagine it was the last thing you wanted to hear, but it's important you take this seriously. Without your ability to sense incoming demons…"

"Yes, I know. I'll be in greater danger. Then again, without Brax and Moore at my side, I can find myself in great danger as well. Are you telling me I'm doomed, John. Is there no way I can win this?"

"No, it just means it's not going to be easy." John looked down and up. "Your mother, Ida, she's a Shadow Light slayer, and she was the one to get all of us slayers together. You look so much like her when she was your age. Well…she went through something similar to what you're going through at your age."

I swallowed. Ida had brought John, Gordon, Marcus, and Kingsley together like I had brought Brax, Asher, and Moore together. Did she have feelings for them all too, like I did with my slayers? At that moment, I felt an intense wave of compassion and sympathy go through me for the woman who gave birth to me and was now lying in a coma somewhere in a hospital in Italy. Was I to follow in her footsteps? Were my slayers to follow in the Shadow Light slayers' footsteps too?

Chapter 15

Moore's Struggle

That night was long and sleepless. The few moments of sleep I managed were filled with dreams of John and Ida. In one dream, I'd come home from school, a normal school little girls go to and are normal. Ida was home, baking as she waited for me. She was happy to see me and greeted me with a big hug and a wet kiss on my brow.

When I pulled out the homework I had to do, she sat right there with me, going over multiplication tables. She was patient and kind, not to mention a good teacher. I felt happy and safe and never wanted to leave.

Waking up from each of these fleeting dreams, however, I felt guilty and ashamed. I knew I'd had the greatest parents and couldn't believe I could even dream of a better life with Ida.

At four o'clock, I could stand it no longer and got out of bed. Looking around my room the guilty and shame I'd felt was amplified. Though our home was modest in comparison to Brax and Moore's, it was a warm and loving home, and a girl could hardly ask for a cooler room. I had a view that skimmed over a few of the neighbors' roofs and a bathroom all my own.

It was far too early to get ready for school, so I went into my private bathroom to take a leisurely bath, something I rarely did. Filling the tub I added a few drops of scented oil, knowing the gentle fragrance would awaken me and help my mood.

Something was wrong and I felt it in my bones. I couldn't shake it off, even as I lit a few candles and set them around the tub, even as I tried to breathe in and relax, my muscles remained tense and tight. I shrugged my robe off my shoulders and dipped my toes into the steaming water.

Just the perfect temperature; hot.

I slid in, letting the heat soothe me and I sunk in until the water rose over my shoulders. Out the window I saw the dim hint of daylight. This was starting as a strange day and I knew the remainder would be just as unusual.

Never an early bird, I'd always clung to my pillow until the last minute. I'd often been caught working late into the night, chasing the kind of demons who didn't enjoy venturing out at night. This often left to difficult mornings.

A red robin landed on the sill of my window and chirped its arrival. Batting its wings in pecked at the glass pane. For a long moment I watched it as it struggled to get inside, wondering what it wanted. I'd long ago heard that a bird crashing into a window was a foreboding sign; a message of death.

I looked into his eyes, wanting to find the message it had for me, but just as quickly as it had appeared, it flew off.

Is this to be the day everything turns upside down? Could I truly be destined to end up like Ida?

Wanting to erase all thoughts, I dunked down until my head was completely submerged. Under the water, I opened my eyes, reveling in the dull silence that enveloped me. The world and worries bobbed away on the surface of the water while I remained safely under until I could no longer hold my breath.

As I popped out of the water, gasping for breath, I felt a surge of revival. Whatever I'd needed to find in the water, it'd come to me and I now felt ready to face this impossible day. With still a few hours to go before I had to head out to school, I dried off, pulled on my favorite jeans and t-shirt then plopped down on the bed to read a bit of the Book of Angels.

John had repeatedly stressed the importance of reading, learning and memorizing as much of it as we could and while I'd poured over much of it with Asher on the plane ride back to the United States, I wanted to have as much of it as possible sink in. I wanted it to become a part of me; something I didn't have to think about…a part of me that was automatic to pull out without thinking.

Certain aspects of Latin still eluded me and I knew that simply learning the words without understanding their meaning was useless. Like John had said, we had to believe what we were saying as we sprinkled Holy Water over the portal.

I skimmed through several of the pages, happy with the amount I was able to understand. Just when I'd reached the section I didn't know as well, I heard Mom's soft steps coming up the stairs. After a light knock on the door, she pushed the door ajar and peaked in.

"Honey, you up?"

In no mood to hide anything from her, I set the Book of Angels on my lap. "Yes, Mom. I'm up. Come in."

"You're up early," she said as she came in.

"I'm sorry. Did my bath wake you up?"

"A little, though I admit I slept pretty lightly all night. I guess John's unexpected visit disturbed me a little more than I would have thought."

"Me, too."

"Look," she said as she gazed at the Book of Angels. "I don't want to keep you from your... duties, but I just wanted to tell you, I've always loved you like you were my own. It took no time at all for me to forget that you weren't my blood. The only thing that constantly reminded me that you weren't mine was..."

"The demon slaying," I interjected.

She chuckled lightly. "You'd think that would be what concerned me, but no. I was fearful for the first few years that John and Ida would come around and claim you.

I think you turned seven before I stopped thinking of that eventuality, before I finally felt secure in my motherhood."

"I'm sorry this has upset you so much."

"Well, now that it's out, I guess it's for the best." She patted my cheek and looked at me with tenderness and love in her eyes. "I'll let you to your things. I just wanted a chance to talk to you alone before you left for the day."

"Thanks, Mom. I'm glad you did."

As she left I heard the slow, almost reluctant steps as she went downstairs then headed for the shower.

It was almost six o'clock and I was amazed the time had gone so fast. I'd gone from being well in advance for the school day to the verge of being late. Grabbing my bag, I pulled it over my shoulder and hurried downstairs for a few bites of breakfast.

While I wolfed down a bowl of Cheerios I heard my father rise and join my mother in the shower. The thought made me smile. They were still so in love with each other, it was inspirational. Would the love I have for either of my slayers end up being the kind that would last forever like the one my parents have? I sighed. Right now I have obstacles to overcome with each of them before I can even think of committing to either. Brax and Moore were becoming full-fledge demons, and Asher was my guardian. To me, they were supposed to be off-limits, but my love for them as friends and companions have blossomed into something else.

Before they came out and I was confronted with another dose of parental love, I shoved my empty bowl into the dishwasher, grabbed an apple and headed off to school.

Before the first class I spotted Brax and though he looked tired, he appeared fine. He looked like himself, smiled, and even seemed to be in a good mood. The only thing that concerned me was his lack of eye contact. Of course he was far down the hall when I spotted him, but he usually saw me from afar and was quick to come to me.

I tried not to let it bother me and headed down to my Science class, hoping to spot Asher on the way. I just had time to see him dash into his Biology class and I had the same impression as I'd had with Brax. He seemed fine, but didn't spot me from a distance.

Shaking my head, I argued I'd come to take their attention for granted.

My morning classes dragged on and it was impossible to concentrate. Though Mr. Meriwether spoke slowly and eloquently, every other thought reverted to the lines I'd read in the Book of Angels that morning.

By the time lunch came around, I realized I'd yet to see Moore. Worried, I hurried to find him but ran into Brax instead.

"Hey," he said with a cockeyed grin. "How was your first night back?"

"Torture."

"John go back to meet your parents?"

"Yeah."

"Must be rough."

There was something odd and distant in his manner of speaking, as though the words flowed from his mouth out of habit but without any conviction.

"How are you doing?" I asked as I reached out to gently touch his arm.

"I had a rough night, too. My uncle's house seemed bigger and emptier than ever. It was cold, dark and... lonely. Though I had to share you with Moore and Asher, I have to admit I was growing accustomed to spending the day with you, waking to see you, going to bed not too far away from you. Maybe one day we'll be able to do that without Moore and Asher."

We stopped talking and simply looked at each other a moment as a dozen students filed by. The air in the school seemed to have changed since we'd last been here and I could sense that in the students. There was something different about them, something in their demeanor, in their stride.

Shaking my head and setting aside my concern, I turned back to Brax.

"I'm sorry if things are a little confusing now. If it helps any, I'm confused as well. I've never felt the tumultuous emotions I have these past months. And with the portal open and…"

"I know, Lux. I'm not asking you to explain or justify your emotions. I know it's not easy. I'm just letting you know where my head is at."

"Mr. Ho would have your head for ending your sentence with a preposition like that."

He chuckled. "Bad habit, I guess. I'm sure he'd forgive me."

"I don't know. He once chastised me in front of the whole class for saying who when I should have said whom."

"Remember when I used to tutor you."

I heard the softness in his voice and was immediately transported to those first days at St. James Academy. He'd seemed so innocent back then.

"I loved those times with you. It helped me with my grades, but it helped me get to know you."

"Tables are turned now. Look at who's giving me English lessons."

It was so good talking about things other then demons and portals. It felt good to just be normal; a boy and a girl, in school, talking about things students should talk about. I wanted to lean into him, and be the flirtatious girl who claws after the handsome jock.

He looked around and I sensed the quiet, normal moment had passed. We were back to demon slayers and gatekeepers.

"I thought it might be a good idea if we got together tonight, go over the Book of Angels, learn the blessings John wants us to learn."

Beaming, I nodded. "I think that'd be great, Brax.

Chapter 16

Falling

Being back in school the next day was a surreal experience. I felt my soul was still back in Italy, trying to plot out how to remedy the situation with the portal and the many demons coming through it. I had no doubt Asher, Brax and Moore felt the same. Our time with Markus, Gordon and John had been enlightening, and, for me, had also changed something deep within my core.

Perhaps it was learning about my relationship to John and the true nature of my relationship with the parents I'd always known, or maybe it was the proximity to such worldly and experienced demon slayers.

Wanting to find Moore, I stopped at my locker to dump my books, hoping to head down the hall in the direction of his locker afterward. I hadn't seen him all day and he'd been strangely quiet the whole flight back.

He'd been moody before, at times creeping off to some dark place within him, but this was worse. I sensed a complete disconnect and it worried me. At the same time, however, I knew it was best for me to keep my distances.

Just before getting back on the plane, we'd had a moment alone in Italy. The scene had been like that of a perfect romance novel; sunset, beautiful music and his warm hand over mine. I wanted to lose myself in him. I'd spent so much of my life being strong, being a warrior, being a fighter; I wanted to spend a moment just being a girl, a woman with a man. I wanted to be free of my demon slayer duties, of the obligations they brought and simply give in to the urges that pulled me to him.

After all the years I'd put in, didn't I deserve at least that? A pleasant moment in Italy with a beautiful man begging to get closer to me? Couldn't I let go, give in, enjoy?

"Why is it I have a feeling things are going to change the moment we get back?" he'd asked as his fingers had tightened around mine.

"I think we've learned a lot, Moore. Markus, Gordon and John gave us all a lot to think about. I think we've learned a lot about what we have to do, here with the demons and the opened portal, but we've also learned about ourselves and our roles here."

He pulled me into his arms. "I don't want to talk about demons and slaying and angels. I want to enjoy this last night here with you. I never want this moment to end. I want to stay here, with you, forever."

Though it'd killed me, I'd had to pull away. The moment he'd pulled me into his arms, I'd felt the darkness that lay deep within him. As much as I wanted to be with him, and as much as it felt good being so close to him, I had to step back and revert to the demon slayer I was.

"I wish I could be the type of girl you want me to be, Moore. The kind of girl who melts into your arms and purrs to your kisses, but…"

"Don't say that," he said, instantly pressing his finger to my lips. "You are exactly the kind of girl I want, and don't ever think differently. You're perfect for me. I love you just the way you are. If anything, I'm the one who is at fault here. I'm the one who is cursed."

Shadow Light: Beautiful Beings Book 3

*****

Staring into my locker now, I'd forgotten what I was there for, the memory of those moments was so strong. The scent of his breath, and the touch of his hand still left a tremor deep inside my gut.

"Hey, Lux."

I turned to see Asher rushing to me and quickly shook off the heat caused by thoughts of Moore.

"Do you have a lunch date yet?"

I chuckled and slammed my locker door shut. Though he fully understood and accepted my reluctance to become involved in any kind of relationship with him, he still kept the door open with that witty smirk of his.

"A lunch date?"

"Yeah," he said with a cock of his brow. "I have a nice tray of lasagna all lined up for you."

"Sounds so romantic." I batted my eyes in an exaggerated fashion. "It's almost like being back in Italy."

"Speaking of Italy," he said. "How's Moore dealing with being back in San Fran? He didn't really seem too much like himself on the flight back."

"Don't know," I said as we maneuvered through a crowd of students who hurried toward the cafeteria. "I haven't seen him yet today and he's given no sign of life since stepping off that plane."

"Worried?" he said as he pushed through the cafeteria door.

I didn't want to have to admit it so I shrugged and left it at that.

"Hmm," he said while patting his belly for effect. "Smells like the lasagna I love."

"You're a bit chipper this morning. What's gotten into you?" I grabbed a tray at the beginning of the lunch counter and waited from my plate of lasagna.

"Though I still have a few questions, I think our trip to Italy was rather fruitful."

"What questions do you still have?"

He looked at me, his eyes telling me to wait until we were alone.

I paid the cashier then led the way to a quiet table out on the patio. The sun was blinding and the heat good on my skin. I still felt suffocated by the time we'd spent in that dank church underbelly and felt a constant need to renew the air in my lungs.

"So," I said once we'd settled at a table. "What are these questions about?"

"We found out how to close the portal, but the thing we still don't know is how to find it."

I nodded thoughtfully as I poked my fork into the cheesy lasagna and pulled up a long stringy line of melted cheese. "We know it's in San Francisco," I said before taking a bite.

"Yeah, but I think we're going to have to narrow it down a bit more than that."

"Any ideas?"

"I woke up early this morning and poured over the Book of Angels. Somewhere in there it mentions finding a place of high activity, and finding a place with plenty of fresh souls."

"Okay, good. So that means we're not looking at an individual home or something like that. This is a larger place; a place that can hold a lot of people." I thought of the places I'd experienced the heaviest amount of activity. "I've seen the most activity at Brax's house or here at school. I don't think they would want to waste too much time and energy preying on the house of a gatekeeper," I muttered.

"Like Brax."

"Yeah, nor would they want to take that big a risk for nothing."

"So that leaves here." He ate his lasagna as if we were talking about remedial soccer, or the night's English essay. His gaze darted around the various picnic tables set here and there then turned to focus on the hundreds of students inside the cafeteria.

"It would make sense," I added, my tone hushed. "After all I was brought here to St. James. I don't think it was an idle move on Dr. Kingsley's part. I mean, look at me. Do I really look like the kind of student who would enroll in such an exclusive school? Never mind be accepted?"

"I think you underestimate yourself too much, but, yeah. I can see what you mean."

"The only reason I'm here is because Dr. Kingsley was on the board."

"I guess it's lucky for us this is all happening while you're still at the age to go to this school."

I chuckled half-heartedly. "I guess you could look at it that way. You know, my whole life I've gone from school to school. I could never stay for more than a month or so."

"Trouble-maker."

"I'll say."

"You really started slaying that young, huh?"

"Two years old," I said with a heavy nod. "This is the longest I've been at the same school."

"Must be because of me," he said with an impish grin.

I looked his way and pointed my fork at him. "You might be onto something there."

"What's your next class?" he said in an idle manner.

"Biology."

"Hmm." He grabbed our empty trays and stood. "Does that help any with the dealing of demons?"

"Not really."

Leaving our trays on the outside garbage can, we then re-entered the cafeteria and made our way back to our lockers.

As we passed in front of the boys' locker room, Brax emerged.

"Not again," Asher said as he took in Brax's disheveled appearance and lost gaze. "I'll be right back." He shot into the locker room.

"You okay?" I asked Brax.

His eyes still slightly glazed, he nodded.

"I was just telling Asher about the whole reason for my being here at St. James."

Again he nodded.

"We suspected the main core of activity is here at St. James and that's why Dr. Kingsley had me enrolled here."

Brax leaned back against the wall and looked like he was about to be ill.

"I mean, I clearly don't fit in here, so why else would I come to a school like this?"

Looking at my shoes, Brax murmured something unintelligible.

"What was that?"

"They're playing with you, aren't they?"

Frowning, I looked into his hazy eyes. "Who? What do you mean?"

"You're just a pawn, a playing piece. You have no real control over what's going on. You're at the mercy of those who make the rules; those who know the game; those who change the game to suit their purposes."

"Brax, you're scaring me. What are you talking about?"

A degree of lucidity came back and he looked me straight in the eye. "It's going to be all right, Lux. You may not be in control, but you're strong and you'll get through it. We're all there to help get you through it."

Pulling me into his arms, he hugged me tight and kissed the top of my head for a long moment. I felt his concern for me in his embrace, but that concern quickly turned into something dark and sinister. I pushed him back and when I looked up, Asher was beside us, his crucifix in hand.

"Asher," I said as I stared at him in disbelief. "What are you doing? Put that down."

"Why don't you ask him what's he doing? Or better yet what he was doing… in there?" He tilted his head toward the locker room door.

I didn't want to ask. I was afraid to ask. Though growing suspicion led me to question Brax's integrity more and more, I didn't want to believe there could truly be anything evil in him.

"Brax?" I said softly.

"Yeah?" His voice resonated with innocence.

"What were you doing in the boys' locker room again? Did you have a game today?" I sounded like a kindergarten teacher and hated it.

"Yeah, Brax," Asher said, sounding more like a prison guard. "I found another drained body in the locker room. Are you going to try to tell me you had nothing to do with it?" He turned to look at me. "There was nobody else in there. I went through every aisle of lockers, threw them all open and looked into every shower stall. The only person I found was the remains of Oliver Sharp."

My heart was split in two; the half that wanted to slay him right there and the half that wanted him to tell me this was all a mistake."

"It wasn't me," Brax said. "And believe me it's not easy. I'm starving for a soul, I'll admit that, but I'm controlling it. As hard as it is, I'm controlling it." He turned to look at me, his eyes imploring me to believe him. "I've been working so hard to fight it off, Lux. It's hard, but I'm managing it. It's not me who took Oliver. It couldn't be."

A group of students passed by, chatting amiably and going about their business as if life was easy and beautiful. How lovely it must be to go through life without a care in the world. How wonderful it must be to have such leisure time to laugh and play. I'd never known that kind of luxury. My leisure time was spent fighting to keep the world free of the demons who preyed on helpless souls.

We all looked to the floor and quieted down the time they passed us by.

"Look," Asher said the moment they'd passed. "I don't know what kind of game you're playing, but this is the second time we find an empty body where you just so happen to have been. You're going to say it's all a coincidence? Well, I don't believe it."

Darkness quickly filled Braxton's eyes. Laying my hand over Asher's arm, I silently begged him to keep quiet. "Coincidences happen," I said. I shot a glance at Asher and looked back at Brax. "No use getting all upset over this. I know you're working hard to keep control and I wouldn't want you to lose that grip on control. Please don't get upset with all this."

"I'm not getting upset," Brax grumbled, sounding more like a petulant child than a demonic teenager.

Still, my gut told me this wasn't good. I was worried about the control he really did have over this. Maybe he was able to control it while he was conscious of his actions, but could the darkness be working through him without his realizing it?

With the portal getting larger and larger, it was a possibility I had to consider... and worry about.

Chapter 17

Lost

"Asher, would you mind giving us a few minutes alone?" I said.

His eyes gave a definite no as an answer, but he nodded all the same. "I'm going to go out and take a look at the field. Maybe I'll find an answer out there."

Brax and I silently watched him walk outside then strolled slowly to the doors Asher had used.

"You know there've been others," Brax said. "Others like Oliver and…"

"Yes," I said. "I heard."

"I wasn't anywhere near them. Some even happened while we were in Italy, so…"

"Okay." I reached out to pat him arm. "I don't think you had anything to do with this. Just bad timing I guess."

Brax kicked an imaginary rock on the hardwood floor. "Yeah, that seems to be following me around lately."

"I'm hoping we'll find the portal soon, Brax. I know this has been hard and I can't imagine what you're living with, but I promise I'll do all I can to get rid of the demon that's growing inside you."

"I know I should be comforted by that, but right now, I'm just sick of the whole thing. I'm exhausted by the constant struggle, by the fighting. I'm fighting myself and it's the worst feeling in the world."

"Please hold on until we find the portal. We know it's around here somewhere."

"Where, in San Francisco? That's not much help." He glared at me, something the Brax I knew was not apt to do.

"No... here, at St. James. We think the portal could be right here; virtually under our noses."

We walked out and the blinding sun that had so warmed my skin moments earlier now seemed to irritate and annoy Brax. He pulled up the collar of his shirt and shielded his eyes with his hand. "Do we really have to come out here?" he said in a plaintive tone. "It's as hot as hell out here today."

I didn't comment on his choice of words, but glanced at Asher who seemed to have found something interesting.

"Hey, you guys." His gaze was intently on the ground just near the doorway that led straight into the boys' locker room. "I think I may have found something."

I stepped forward, but stopped when I noticed that Brax had remained behind. "Aren't you going to come?" I said.

He stared at me and shoved his hands in his pockets. "Something doesn't smell right out here."

I sniffed the air and realized he was right and it wasn't the smell of sweaty lacrosse players. It was something more vile, more sinister. Nonetheless, I walked back to him, took him by the hand and led him to Asher's side. "What do you have?"

"Look." Asher pointed to the ground. "Have you ever seen anything like that before?"

A look of fear and pain instantly creased Brax's face as he looked at the dark hole in the ground. Barely a foot in diameter, the hole looked like a void, an empty space that swirled in an endless abyss.

"That's it," Brax whispered. "I can feel it to my bones...that's the portal to hell."

The scent was unmistakable. Even with my weakened senses, the pull toward the darkness was immense, almost insurmountable. I'd felt like this so many times in the past; heavy and dizzy.

"I can barely inhale, the smell of sulfur and ashes is so great," Asher commented as he turned away from the stench.

Before I could turn to question Brax about what he knew of this portal, he threw himself onto his knees and raised his fists into the air as a plaintive cry echoed out onto the empty playing field.

I felt his crumbling soul; felt I was losing him. As weakened as he'd become these past weeks, he now seemed on the verge of losing whatever remained of his control.

"Brax," I said as I set my hand to his trembling shoulder.

He was beside himself with grief, with loss, before he'd even lost the fight entirely. He was giving up, I could feel it.

"You can't stay here, Brax."

Looking up at me, his eyes were bereft of all emotion; empty; a deep void.

"You have to leave San Francisco before it's too late. You must leave until we're able to close the portal."

His eyes remained glazed and confused.

"Do you understand me, Brax? Do you hear me? You have to leave."

"No," he muttered softly. "I can't. There's so much to do. I have you to protect. Don't make me go."

"You don't understand. It's too dangerous for you here. You can't stay this close to the portal. The hold it has over you is getting stronger and stronger. You have to get away."

"What about you? You can't stay."

"It doesn't have the same pull on me that it has on you. You're vulnerable. You know you are. You feel it, don't you? Just now?"

As though suddenly feeling weak, he stood, pulled back his shoulders and gazed down at me. "I can still fight it. I may have allowed myself a temporary moment of weakness, but I still have some fight left in me, Lux."

"Please, Brax. Don't fight me on this. If you remain here you'll only make it harder for us to fight the demonic forces of this portal. I'll be too preoccupied with your safety. You should go to Europe."

"No. I don't want to go back there."

"Then maybe go to New York, or anywhere on the East coast. Just get out of San Francisco; out of California."

Despite his desire to remain strong and argue with me, I saw him crumble to the ground again."

"The pull is unbelievable. I never thought it could be like this. I thought I was so strong. I thought I could fight this, no matter what. How am I going to manage out East without you?"

"You'll do fine." I helped him back up and led him away from the portal.

Several yards away he was finally able to straighten up and walk on his own. "I hate that I can't deal with this on my own."

"I know, but this is what's best for all of us. Please. This is the only way we'll be able to close the portal and beat them."

"I hate the thought of leaving you completely alone."

"I won't be alone, Brax. Asher and Moore are here with me."

"That's even worse." His eyes softened and his lips parted. "Come with me, Lux. Leave all this demon slaying business to Asher and Moore and come away with me. We could both escape all of this and…"

"There's no more time to waste, Brax. Go! Now!" I tried to bring a sense of urgency to my words. I wanted to shake him out of this lethargy.

I glanced back at Asher who stared at the portal, mesmerized by its power.

"I have to go back to Asher before he succumbs to the pull as well. Please, Brax. I'll ask you one last time, leave the demon fighter and closing of the portal to us and go where you'll be safe."

Brax raked his fingers through his hair. "Okay, you're right."

The light finally came back into his eyes; the light of the Braxton I'd first met.

"Thanks, Lux. I think if you hadn't intervened, I would have lost the last of the fight I had in me, the pull was that strong."

"I'll contact you as soon as everything is clear."

"Don't you think I should bring Moore with me? Isn't he as vulnerable as I am?"

I knew he was right, but was reluctant to have Moore so far away from me. It didn't make sense and I knew I had to put his safety before my desire to have him at my side throughout this ordeal.

"I haven't seen him since we got back from Italy. If you can find him... if you can contact him and tell him what's going on... yes. Bring him with you. Tell him I told you to leave with him and to stay away until Asher and I have completely contained the portal."

Though he nodded, I could see he was bothered by my concern for Moore.

"You'd prefer he stayed here with you, don't you?"

I heard the pain in his voice and didn't have the heart to add to it. "Moore is just as susceptible to the forces here. We need to keep our numbers up if we're going to survive this. We can't afford to let Moore turn into a full-fledged demon like Shayne. You do understand that, don't you?"

He nodded.

"You have his number?"

He flipped on his phone, checked his list of contacts then muttered, "Yeah."

"Then hurry up and find him, then leave."

Before he could argue further, I turned away and returned to Asher and the portal.

"It's too late," I heard Brax call from behind me.

No, I thought with a sharp pang to my heart. I turned to glance back on him, but my gaze halted at the boys' locker room door.

"He's already here at St. James," Brax went on.

The door opened and Moore stepped out. I wanted to shout and tell him to hurry back inside, but he rushed out and headed to the side of the field where Asher stood. My voice remained trapped in my throat.

"Moore," I finally managed to croak, but he didn't hear me and continued walking to Asher. "Don't."

The scene played out like a disaster scene from a movie and I felt helpless to stop it. He seemed so determined to make it to that portal, and I doubted Asher would be able to stop him. With a new thrust of adrenaline, my feet carried me across that field with more speed than I would have thought myself capable of, but my eagerness left me clumsy and I tripped over my own feet and landed flat on my face.

Nose deep in turf, I heard thundering footsteps pass me by. Feeling as though I'd lost the battle before it'd even begun, I struggled to get to my knees only to see Brax run by and hurry to Moore who now stood shoulder to shoulder with Asher.

"Brax, you can't," I shouted.

"I can't just stand by and do nothing, Lux. Moore was there and helped me deal with this whole demon thing. Now it's my turn to do what I can."

My heart was torn. I knew I'd never make it to Moore's side in time, and I desperately wanted Brax to get there and save him, but Brax... He wouldn't be able to survive being so close to the portal without someone there to save him.

Several yards still separated him from Moore. I had to try and stop him.

Getting to my feet I chased him. "Brax, stop. You can't save him. You have to save yourself."

"He's far more entrenched in all this than I am. He's more vulnerable. He has nothing to fight with."

Reaching him, I grabbed his arm and pulled him to a stop. "This is suicide, Brax. Go back. Get off the school property. I'll take care of Moore." I glanced past him and saw Moore slumped toward Asher. He seemed so weak, so hypnotized. I could barely see a shadow of the guy I'd come to love so much; the man who'd touched me so deeply. With a deep sense of nausea sweeping over me, I looked to Brax.

"I'm the gatekeeper, remember. I can fight the powers of the portal off better than he can. I know you're strong, Lux, and I know you want to deal with this your own way, but there's only so much you can do on your own. Moore isn't in a good place of mind right now. You don't know what he's capable of. You don't know how he'll behave once you get within arms' reach."

"I'm afraid for you, Brax. Moore is just as apt to reach out and hurt you. If anything even more so."

He smirked and patted my cheek affectionately. "I don't think I've ever seen you so worried about me. It's kind of nice, but the timing could be a bit better. Come on. Are you going to come and fight this with me or are you going to stay there and argue with me all day?"

I stared into the eyes of a new young man, a man I'd never seen before. He no longer had the glazed expression of a man lost to the demons. He was in full control and knew what he had to do.

"I am the descendant of Shadow Light gatekeeper after all," he said with pride. "You can't go wrong fighting at my side. Think about it, either we stay together and fight this thing, or we all fall to the ground, one by one."

"Okay, you win. I'm with you."

"Then get your fighting game on and let's shut this portal down once and for all."

Chapter 18

Collision of Souls

The ground beneath our feet shook and the urgency of the situation chilled me. It was all coming to this; the years of fighting, the years of learning how to dominate the demonic influences that constantly threatened to over humanity.

I saw the look of horror on Brax's face and questioned if we were really up to such a battle.

"This is going to be big."

At the far corner of the school building, a small group of students emerged, adding a degree of difficulty to the battle that lay ahead. It was important to keep them out, the keep them from becoming involved, and to keep them from being killed by the very demons that could arouse their curiosity.

A few sophomores looked our way, the girls eyeing Brax while a few guys looked at me. "We can't let them get close to the portal. It'll become a feeding frenzy."

We both looked at Asher and Moore. The fight had already begun and while Asher held his own, Moore seemed to struggle more and more.

"I'll hurry over and divert them. I'll find some reason to send them running back inside. You go and dive in there," I ordered Brax.

He nodded and hurried to help Asher and Moore, and I turned my attention to the young onlookers who were quickly approaching.

"Hey, you're the senior hottie I've been hearing about," a sophomore said as he approached me with a cool stride that didn't match the pimply faced kid that he was. "I've been meaning to reach out and get to know you."

"Calling me a senior hottie isn't exactly going to do it. Why don't you guys go back inside and try to devise a better pick up line?"

"What's going on? It looks like a major fight over there."

"None of your business..." I said in a harsh tone, but I instantly saw that it wasn't really the way to go. The girls glared at me and the guys seemed more defensive than obliged. Pulling out the tart in me, I played the delicate damsel in distress card and hoped they went for it. "You know, on second thought, I am starting to feel a little flushed by the sun. It is getting pretty hot out here and it's affecting me more than I would have thought. Can one of you guys go in and get me something long and cool to drink? Maybe an iced-tea with plenty of ice. I'd sure appreciate it. I'd be forever grateful."

Another sophomore scrambled forward. "I'll get you whatever you need, babe."

Oh, brother, I thought with a deep desire to shake my head, but I simply smiled my prettiest smile and said. "I won't forget you." I patted his smooth cheek.

"Come on, guys." The shorter of the two guys obviously had the role of ring leader because the others followed him without saying a word.

With the coast now clear I turned my attention to the battle ahead. I turned to see Asher and Brax fighting hard while it was hard to tell which side Moore was on. He was losing control. Even from this distance, I could see him struggling.

I reached them just as three demons circled Asher and tried to pull him down. Awed by his power and prowess, I froze and watched him for a moment, then got in the game. They were coming out so fast, I could barely understand how Asher and Brax had managed so well. Moore was of no help and showed signs of becoming like Shayne.

He hurried to me and my fingers twitched to find my crucifix.

"You have to help me, Lux. They're pulling me in." His eyes flared red then yellow, then back to red. In a flash he turned and slayed two demons with one quick motion, but when he turned to me again, his eyes still retained the demonic influence that was taking over him.

"You're doing great," I said, despite my reservations. "So long as you fight and slay the demons instead of fighting with them. Don't give up, Moore. We're this close to our goal. Stay strong."

At that very moment a demon came from behind me and pulled me to the ground. It was all over me, keeping me from reaching for my crucifix. Closer and closer it came until it's putrid breath burned my skin.

Moore jumped in, tearing the demon to shreds with such ferocity, I couldn't help but be afraid in the very same instant I was proud.

"Thanks," I shouted over the cries of battle. "I owe you one."

The ground shook again, sending both slayers and demons to the ground. The portal grew wider and wider, and the number of demons reached the threshold of manageability. We were going to lose, I thought as I looked at the impossible number of demons.

Moore stayed close to me, helping me and keeping me safe whenever I struggled. Every demon he slayed gave me hope for his soul.

"Watch it," I shouted as a small army of demons rushed toward him.

They recognized him as one of their own and seemed caught off guard as they looked into his eyes. Moore used this to his advantage. He murmured something to them, something that encouraged them to let their guard down.

I grinned as he played with their twisted minds, their twisted sensibilities. Just as they released him and prepared to attack Brax, Moore pounced on them and they were quickly slain before they even knew what had hit them.

"Whatever you're losing in your ability to control these demonic forces, you certainly are making up for it with deceit. That was absolute genius."

Another band of demons marched toward us, but this time they weren't willing to listen to anything Moore had to say. They forged on, attacking him and leaving him barely able to fight them off. While I was kept busy fighting, Moore faltered and fell to his knees. I wanted to throw my crucifix at the demons on his back. My heart tore in two as the demons pinned him down and prepared to finish him off.

A demon had me on my back fighting to get him off me. I was useless and completely unable to help him.

Tears filled my eyes as I shut them to the awful scene playing out before me. I couldn't bear to see him finally taken by the dark side, but hearing a distinctive grunt in the melee, I opened my eyes to see Brax joining Moore in the battle.

I was touched by his actions. Knowing how much he hated Moore and knowing how he wanted nothing more than to have Moore out of my heart, it must have been so tempting to just let him shrivel up and die, but there he was, fighting with all he had.

Fighting the demons with added fervor, I felt a sudden lightness in my heart. We were going to win this. I could see it reflected in Brax's eyes. He'd taken on the role of gatekeeper and was serious about the role. I loved him all the more for it. These past few days it'd been so easy to simply assume my attraction to him was purely physical.

I'd seen just moments earlier how girls in school saw his beauty, but I'd also seen just how profound his beauty ran. For him to put aside his feelings in order to do what was right… it made me realize what kind of man he was, what kind of man he was becoming.

If anything were to happen to him, to any of them, I'd never be able to live with it. I'd grown so close to all of them. As I looked at all of them, I thought back to when I'd first met them, before they'd known who they really were, what their roles were, and what their capabilities were.

As another demon went up in a puff of smoke, I shot a glance at Moore and Brax again. They were a beautiful team, fighting in sync, in perfect harmony. One could have thought they were both parts of the same being they were so uniform in their manner and force.

It shouldn't have come as such a surprise. They'd been friends before I'd come along to St. James Academy; long before I came to San Francisco. They'd been the kind of buddies who sat together for lunch and went to one another's house for fun.

A sudden and deep pang of guilt struck me in the gut as I realized I was the cause of their rift. From the very first moment I spoke to Moore, Brax had changed toward him. Slaying another demon I thought of that first and instant attraction I'd had for Brax.

Strange how things had shuffled around, changed, twisted and changed again. Just as my heart had changed, so had Brax.

A demon rushed me and pushed me into a small group of large and fierce demons. I slayed two, but three more tackled me and sent me to the ground. Asher hurried over and dealt with them fast enough.

"How you holding up?" he asked.

"I'm getting breathless, but holding in there. How long can this go on?"

"I'm beginning to think indefinitely. How long can we go on?"

I jutted my chin toward Brax and Moore. "There seem tireless together. They're like a machine... a finely tuned machine that doesn't miss a beat. If anything the demons must be starting to wonder how long they'll be able to keep up."

"They keep coming and they're stronger."

"I know," I said with a proud grin. "But so are they."

I looked at Asher, his cocky grin aimed at me. "Then I better get moving if I'm going to have you look at me with that kind of pride."

Playfully slapping his arm with my fingertips, I slayed another demon with my free hand.

Asher was the perfect guardian for me. As much as I'd appreciated and loved Lothario my whole youth, although Lothario had been the best guardian a young girl could hope for, Asher was the perfect ally for this stage in my life. I needed him, and he knew it.

I glanced back at Moore. From what Lothario had told me when I'd first arrived in San Francisco, I was to meet people who'd be on my team. I'd expected someone like Asher and I'd expected someone like Braxton, but Moore... I hadn't expected someone like him on my team.

So where did he really fit in? Was he merely on my team, or was there more?

The dream, I thought as I dealt with two demons at once. The moment they blew up in smoke I stopped and turned to look at Moore.

Those dreams I'd had so many times; that mysterious appearance in those dreams. Could it be him? Could that be the part Moore had in all this? From the very first moment I'd met him, he'd reached out to me, he'd demanded my help, even if it wasn't in an obvious way.

I was his last hope, I thought with pride and sadness. I couldn't let him down. No matter what happened, I couldn't let him down.

Another blast of demons stormed through the portal, streaming out with speed that left us all scrambling to keep up. Through the puffs of smoke and ash, it became virtually impossible to see each other and keep up with the actions of one another.

"Lux," Moore shouted as he waved his hands about to get my attention. Fighting off a stream of demons, he made his way closer to me, "Remember what John and Gordon said?"

They'd told us plenty. "What exactly are you talking about?"

"The Holy Water."

"Yeah." I pressed my crucifix to another demon and swore it be gone. "They said it would help us in a situation like this. Obviously we didn't expect to find the portal so fast. None of us had time to get even near a church and get any."

"You underestimate me, my dear Lux. I know what you must have been thinking since we've arrived. That I'd given up. That I'd gone into hiding to face this curse alone. I'll admit I was tempted for a few moments. When we got off the plane and everyone went their separate ways, I'd never felt so alone in my life. I was miserable and hopeless. This curse is immense and I couldn't imagine how I could ever get rid of it. I had to give myself a chance. I had to give us a chance"

I looked at him and was pleased to see the Moore I'd come to love. He was completely there, his eyes clear and his soul intact, but for how long. I knew he couldn't be rid of the curse yet and could only hope this new optimism stayed with him until he was cured.

"That's where I was this morning. I hurried to my parish church and got some. "

"Enough to close the portal," I shouted as I slayed two more demons.

"A few gallons. It should be enough to do the trick." With one quick slice in the air, he terminated a half dozen demons and came to my side. His eyes twinkled with that mischief I'd come to love and I was pleased to learn I wouldn't have to slay him. He seemed stronger than ever and I could have almost sworn he'd grown in height and in breadth.

"Where is it?" I said.

He pressed a quick kiss to my lips and hugged me for a sweet moment. "I had no idea where the portal could be, but I had a feeling it would be here on the school grounds somewhere. I left the gallons in my car."

Just then two dozen or so demons charged us and we were torn apart and forced to battle. Moore took care of virtually all of them, leaving me to slay only a few minor, small demons. The task was easier with him at my side. In all my years of slaying demons, I'd never felt this rush of excitement before; this rush of accomplishment. We were protecting vulnerable students from the worst of demons coming through the St. James portal. We were saving souls, and it was worth fighting for, despite being tired and outnumbered.

When they'd all been dealt with, Moore shouted, "Here," and tossed me the keys to his car. "I wish I'd known where the portal was. I would have brought my car straight here, but I left it in the student parking lot."

"Okay," I said as I grabbed the keys. "I'll hurry and go get it. Keep them busy and make sure none of them follow me." I ran across the field as fast as I could and opened the boys' locker room door. The student parking lot was clear on the other side and I'd have to cut through the whole school to get there.

I raced through the locker room and emerged in the hall, only to face the pimply sophomore who stood there with my iced tea.

"Hey," he said with a pleased grin. "Couldn't wait to have me bring it out, you had to come in and find me yourself."

"Sorry," I said as I rushed by him. "Change of plans."

"Hey." The pleased grin changed into an angry scowl as he let the iced tea fall to the floor and grabbed my wrist. He pulled it back and threw me to the wall. "Just because you're a senior doesn't give you the right to just play around with me like that."

Though he was clearly a few years younger than me, he was just as tall as I was, though still with the frame of a boy.

"Look, something came up and I have to go. It's nothing personal."

"Yeah, it's never anything personal. You hot senior girls think you run the school and that you can do whatever you want. Well, it's gonna stop here. I laid down three and a half bucks for that stupid iced-tea. The least you can do is show a little gratitude."

I reached into my jean pocket and pulled out a ten dollar bill. "Here." I tossed it at him. "Knock yourself out."

He kept me pinned to the wall, unwilling to let go.

"I'll give you one last chance to release me," I said in a foreboding tone. "I don't have time for this."

"Oh, yeah. Then what? You're big bad friends are going to come beat me up?"

"No," I said. "I will." I knocked my forehead to his and he reeled back, cursing and holding his head. "You better start treating women better because we aren't attracted to the crap you're spewing. Want to get a girl to like you? Treat her with respect. Gotta go!"

"Witch," he shouted.

He tried to grab my wrist again, but I dodged him and hurried down the hall. Chasing me, he shouted obscenities at me the whole way.

"I don't have time for this," I muttered. Gave him some advice on how to get girls to like him, and that's what I get. Oh well…I had an open portal to deal with and here was this kid was begging for trouble.

When he continued to pursue me, I had no choice but to make it clear I wasn't playing around. I grabbed him by the neck, shoved him to the wall and set my meanest scowl. "I need you to get off my back, right now, or someone's going to get hurt, and I can guarantee you, it's not going to be me."

His jaw dropped and though he quickly tried to hide his fear, it was clear in his eyes… my message had gotten through. I let him go and hurried down the hall and exited in the students' parking lot. The lot that was usually filled with bright red sports cars, yellow hummers and silver luxury cars now seemed filled with virtually every kind of SUV… all of them black, just like Moore's.

"Damn it," I grumbled under my breath. "Is my luck ever going to turn?"

I beeped his car, hoping it would respond from not too far away. The weak beep sounded clear across the lot, but at least I had a hit. It was off toward the left. I ran through the rows of cars until I was finally able to narrow it down to a short row of SUVs. I beeped, beeped again and beeped one final time before finally finding the one car that matched the key Moore had given me.

Getting into the massive vehicle, I started the car and hurried out of my spot, only to get blocked by a group of students heading to another black SUV. They took their time and blocked the way. Nudging closer and closer, I hoped they'd hear the sound of the engine and move out of the way, but they continued without a care in the world.

I'd have to wait.

Well… I was losing patience and those demons weren't going to wait. Setting my palm to the horn, I revved the engine menacingly.

The two guys continued to walk on, not even glancing back, while the girls turned back, grimaced and went on as if nothing was urgent.

I pressed the horn again and edged closer to their heels.

"Hey, what's the rush?" one of the girls said as the bumper of the SUV brushed against her.

They finally reached their SUV and moved unhurriedly out of the way, glaring at me the entire time.

With tires screeching against the parking lot asphalt, I raced out of the lot and took the small back road that led quickly to the field out back. Even at a distance I could see the smoke and ash. I could also smell the sulfur, and knew it was going to be bad.

But as I drove around, another problem arose. As much as I wanted to, my luck just seemed to refuse to change.

There was no way of driving anywhere near the field. All the fences were closed and locked. The entrance closest to the school building, usually used to let team members on and off the bus was barred by three large cement cubes.

I looked at the guys at the far end of the field. Though they still had minimal control, demons swarmed everywhere. It was just a matter of time before they found an entrance into the school and devoured as many students as they could.

If I couldn't find an entrance into the lacrosse playing field, I'd have to make one. Backing up enough to give me time to speed up, I then gunned it and headed straight into the locked gate. The chain popped open with barely a touch of resistance and soon I was careening across the field on my way to the guys.

"Moore," I shouted as I got out of the SUV. "I got it." I punched the button that popped open the back door and hurried to grab a few gallons.

He disintegrated the demons on his back and came to my side. "What took you so long? For a minute there I thought you'd abandoned us."

"You know I'd never do that," I scolded. "It just seemed that every student in school seemed hell bent on keeping me from getting here."

"Well, the important thing is that you made it. Let's bring as many bottles as we can to the edge of the portal.

John and Gordon said we needed to pour it all around the portal."

I handed him the two gallons I had and reached up to cup his cheeks. "You really came through, Moore. None of us even took the time to go out and get the Holy Water we so desperately need." I kissed him, hard and proud. My heart was pounding and I was filled with adrenaline. Moore looked too good to be true, and I felt like I had to let him know now. If anything happened to either of us, I wanted him to know. "I think it's about time I told you, Moore... I love you."

His brow creased into a confused frown for a moment then his face lit up with pure joy. I knew he'd been waiting so long to hear me say it, and I knew it was time. I realized right then just how much I truly loved him and I knew that hearing me say it out loud would give him even more reason to fight.

Before I could back away, he leaned into me and kissed me back. His kiss was hungry, but cut short by the dire situation we were in. "You certainly make a guy work awfully hard before he can deserve hearing those words." He kissed me again. "I love you, too, Lux. You're the only one I've ever loved with evey core of my body and soul."

"Great," I said with a beaming smile. "Now let's get that portal closed once and for all."

We turned to head to the portal, only to find almost a hundred demons blocking the way.

"I think they know what's coming," Moore said.

"Look, I'll create a distraction, keep them busy while you go and pour all this over the portal."

"I can't."

"What?" I turned to him, stunned and fearful he'd turned suddenly dark. "What do you mean? Why can't you?"

"Lux, it's Holy Water. I'm cursed with the devil. If I even get a drop of this stuff on me, I'm...."

"Oh, yeah, right. Sorry. I hadn't thought of that." I smiled sheepishly, feeling foolish for not having thought of that possibility, and feeling guilty for suspecting him of having succumbed to the powers of his curse.

"I'll create the distraction and you handle the Holy Water," he said. "Beside, I'm not even sure I could have handled being that close to the portal. The pull is strong enough even from this distance. I don't know how I'd be able to handle standing right on the edge.

"Okay, you're right."

Moore grabbed my wrist and looked me in the eyes. "I'd do anything for you, Lux, anything to be with you. I will beat them, I'll beat this curse and I'll be the man you need me to be."

"You are the man I need you to be now, Moore. Don't forget that." With difficulty, I grabbed the two gallons he had and prepared to rush to the portal the moment the path was cleared.

Though Brax was kept busy with a large number of demons, Asher caught wind of what we were up to and joined in the battle Moore took up. Before long, I had a clear path.

Chapter 19

The Deception of Demons

With a clear path to the portal, I finally saw an end to all this chaos. We were going to win. But my thrill of victory was short-lived. A small band of demons had found the entrance to the school. Brax tried to fight them off and for a moment I questioned what my next move should be; run to him to stop the demons from entering, or hurry to pour the Holy Water over the portal.

"Lux," Brax called out. "Two of them made it in."

I couldn't let another student fall prey to these demons. Setting down the jugs of Holy Water, I rushed to the door and hurried after the stray demons, but once inside it seemed my ability to see them had vanished. Outside in the bright sunlight I'd been able to catch their shadows, their movements and in some cases even see them clearly, but now they were mere clouds of dust, vague, dispersed and difficult to follow.

Concentrating as hard as I could, I spotted them, not only the two I'd seen enter, but four more. They'd all turned down the hall that led to the auditorium. Thankfully the lunch hour was over and few students were left wandering the halls.

I turned the corner and found a strong young man pinned back to the wall. At first I couldn't see the cause for his odd posture, but then saw the glimmer of a demon; not only a demon, but a beautiful being. Cast in the disguise of a tall, slim blond with hair that flowed well past her waist, she was an angelic vision of purity.

Exactly the disguise a demon would want.

My crucifix high and ready I hurried to her. She turned to me, her blue eye wide, innocent and alluring. For a moment, I thought I might be mistaken, but then she smiled and I saw the sharp little teeth that gave away her true being and her true hunger.

No sooner had I pulled her off her victim and slayed her that I spotted a young guy, delectably handsome, shoving a girl into the lockers. His lips were just inches from her lips as she struggled to get free. When I reached him, I snaked my arm around his neck and pulled him back, then pressed my crucifix to his brow.

With that done, I turned to find four more roaming the halls and looking for fresh meat. Two of them quickly cornered two young girls who looked positively petrified. These demons didn't even bother posing as beautiful beings, but simply approached the girls with their true demonic features.

One of the girls screamed and tried to run away, but was quickly caught by the smaller demon.

"What in the world are you?" the taller girl asked.

"You dream come true," the bigger demon snarled.

"Dream on," the tall girl said as she pulled out a bottle of pepper spray and doused both demons. They sprinted down the hall, shouting and screeching as they went. They passed in front of me, but I doubt they even saw me standing there.

For a moment the demons were caught off guard and they stumbled, but when they followed after the girls, I slipped my foot out and tripped one of them then managed to quickly slay him.

Shadow Light: Beautiful Beings Book 3

Seeing me, the other demon slipped into an empty classroom. I chased after him, but the room was silent and still. I rushed to the window to see if he'd slipped out.

I'm losing my sight again, I thought, and in that moment he jumped on my back and I almost lost my balance. I twirled around, more a reflex of his jump than a planned move, but the effect was positive all the same. Shoving my back into the wall with as much force as I could, I managed to rid myself of his bulk and slay him.

The moment I ran out of the room I heard a shout coming for down the hall. In a mad dash for the girls' bathroom, I held my crucifix up and ready. How many more could there be? Had many slipped into the school without my noticing them?

The girls' bathroom echoed with the cries of several terrified girls, but I could see nothing but several pairs of feet under the stall doors. As the screams continued to fill the air, I jumped up and climbed over the door. Lacking grace I threw myself on the demon and slayed him, then quickly bolted out of the stall only to climb in another and another.

Leaning back on the sink I faced the three girls I'd just saved. Their eyes were wide with wonder and fear.

"Hopefully that's the last of them," I muttered and quickly ran out.

I had to get back to the field and close the portal and this would never end.

To my horror, I emerged onto the field to find the portal bigger than ever. The demons were now monumental in size.

One of them stood out among the rest. Over two feet taller than the tallest of them, he towered over every demon and made my demon slayers look like second graders.

Chapter 20

Monsters at the Gate

Osidian. For years I'd known of this demon, this monster among monster. I'd long thought he was a myth, a fabrication of the angels to keep demon slayers like me ready for the worst eventuality. And now, here I was facing him when there was already far too much opposition.

I wanted to weep for the immensity of the task ahead. In all my years of slaying demons, I'd never had to face such a lopsided battle. I felt suddenly weak and unable to master the demon slaying tactics I'd spent all my life perfecting. Could it be that all of these years, all the hard work would end up being for nothing? Would the demons really win over?

Osidian approached me, a knowing gleam in his eyes.

I refused to show the fear I felt. If I was going to go down, it would be through a fierce battle, not a feminine screech of terror. But as he got closer and closer, the true immensity of his size made it clear I would not be able to fight him.

Even if he didn't fight me back at all, there was no way I could get closer enough to him to push my crucifix to his black, leathery skin. A scream began to form at the back of my throat, despite my willingness to remain strong.

I needed help; Asher or Brax or Moore… help me.

But my shout was a silent prayer that went nowhere. Osidian continued his approach, unhurried, unworried and rather pleased with himself.

"I've heard a lot about you, Lux."

"And I you."

We stared at each other, sizing each other up, analyzing each other.

"Let's see if all I've heard, all I've been warned about has been true," he said with a challenging sneer.

"Not so fast."

Stunned, I turned to find John standing several feet behind me.

"How…?" The question that begged to be asked stuck on my lips. It didn't matter now how or why he was here. The important thing is that he was.

"Osidian has eluded me for far too long," he said with a wink. He turned to Osidian. "Haven't you?"

"This isn't quite your end of the jungle, John. Don't you have a Franciscan monk to save somewhere?"

"I do believe it is you who is playing in the wrong end of the jungle, Osidian. Though I may have been stationed elsewhere for all these years, this is a battle that I have always sworn to win. Added to that is the very prey you've chosen to pursue." John gave me a knowing glance, causing Osidian to frown.

"Yes, Osidian," John went on. "This is my daughter, Lux. You didn't really think I'd just sit back in Italy while you opened the portal here and made a shriveled crisp out of her, did you?"

"The truth is I didn't really think about you one way of the other. The portal is open, John. Despite all your little teachings and all your precise planning, it's open. Neither you nor Gordon nor Markus could stop it. And that Dr. Kingsley… if anything he was always your weakest link. You're better off without him."

"When the world is rid of your kind, Osidian, I'll be better off." John pounced on Osidian with surprising force.

I fell back and watched as the two masters battled it out, each giving back what the other offered. Just when I thought John was a goner, he'd rebound and send Osidian reeling back. And just when I thought the fight was finally over and Osidian was about to turn to dust, he pushed John back and was ready for another round.

I knew this was the only opportunity I was going to get to close the portal. I reached for the jugs of Holy Water and turned to the ever widening portal. As I pulled off the cap of the jugs, I heard and even felt the cry that came from Osidian. My attempts to close the portal had rendered him all the more ferocious and savage.

With a quick and uncompromising swipe of his claws he sent John flying back into the wall. His eyes remained wide with horror for a moment then he slumped down to the ground.

I wanted to cry out, but there was no time. Osidian descended on me like a wolf onto a sick fawn. All he needed was a quick flick of his finger and he'd rid me of my crucifix. I was helpless and he knew it.

With the jug of Holy Water still in my hands, I splashed some into my palm and tried to spray Osidian, but he just snickered at my feeble attempt.

"And to think you're John's daughter," he said with a condescending sneer. "I would have thought he'd raised you smarter than that. I would have thought he'd trained you better than that. Turns out you're no better than all the simpleton demon slayers who do well with the light stuff, but can't deal with the real demons who threaten to take over."

With those wise words, he slashed his claws out at me, cutting through the skin of my shoulder. I didn't even have time to utter a cry of pain before another lashing came. I stood up and blocked the next punch he threw at me, but its force made me fall to the ground. He was immediately on me, while I brought my legs in to hurl all my strength against him, sending him back where he knocked jugs of Holy Water to the ground. On hearing the wail of pain and horror from surrounding demons, I knew the jugs were spilling in the right direction. They were spilling Holy Water directly into the portal.

Osidian was not done with me, and he got up with a fury and rushed me with a speed I've never seen a demon possessed before. "You have slained many of us since you were just a mere babe. Now it is time for you to pay," he snarled, his eyes turning red. Osidian's claws ripped through my jacket and sliced the skin of my arm, but I still managed to kick over the few remaining jugs on the ground. The cries of fury and rage rose into the air as the flow of demons dwindled down to nothing and the demons left out on the field were soon to be trapped with no way of returning from where they'd come. I stumbled up and tried pouring more holy water around the portal. With my last strength and breath, it was the only way to close the portal off. Moore and Brax couldn't do it, and Asher was too far from the portal. I did not have much time.

I made it almost completely through the rest of the portal perimeter when I felt a sharp burning pain suddenly hit me like a block of brick. It was so intense, I dropped the holy water jug I was holding and crumbled to the ground.

I felt something wet and warm drip down my clothes and could barely see it was red. Blood. My own.

Suddenly, I couldn't hear anything, and my vision became fainter and fainter.

"Lux!" a male's voice called. It was Moore, and he was running to me, his face looking so worried. Asher was right behind him.

Then I saw it, but I couldn't scream. I had no voice. It felt numb, paralyzed. Osidian was behind Moore, and as the portal was closing, I saw Moore desperately trying to get to me, but he was stopped. Osidian had grabbed hold of him, and before the portal could close, Osidian pushed Moore in.

"Lux, I love you!" Moore cried, his face looking shocked with what was happening.

Tears were streaming down my face along with my blood, making my shirt wet with blood and tears. I couldn't breathe. I couldn't cry out that I loved him too.

Asher was trying to grab Moore's hand, but it was too late, and Asher couldn't get pulled in. As he turned away from the portal, another hand reached out to grab Moore's. It was Brax's hand.

Brax looked over at me, his face grim, but determined. He held onto Moore's hand with all his strength. It wasn't enough, and he was falling into the portal with Moore. Asher leaped onto Brax's legs, trying to anchor him and keep him from falling in further, but Asher was being pulled in, too.

I was slowly fading. As I clung to the remaining threads of consciousness that remained, I was distantly aware of John finally bringing Osidian to his knees. As the portal closed, John took out a flask of holy water and shoved it into Osidian's mouth, causing the demon to burst into flames. I wanted to smile, to celebrate the victory, but one look from John's face, and I knew something was terribly wrong.

That was when I reached up and felt my neck. My throat had been ripped out, and I was dying.

Epilogue

Consciousness came back in tiny wavelets, letting me hear the goings on around me, but not allowing me to respond. It was a frustrating no man's land. But even more frustrating than my intermittent consciousness was my shattering sense of defeat. In all my life I'd never felt so powerless. We closed the portal and John killed Osidian, but something felt different. There was pain and an overall feeling of heaviness surrounding me.

Through the grief and pain, I heard Asher mumbling as he wept. He called out my name, though I couldn't make out what he was saying.

"I'm so sorry," he said, finally sounding coherent and intelligible. "I tried, Lux. I really did. I wanted nothing more than to save you; to save all of them. And now it's all lost. What am I going to do now?"

I felt his hand over mine, his fingers wrapping around mine and crushing them in a grip that was painful. "I know I've never been the best of friends with Moore or

Brax, but you have to believe me. I would have done anything to save them. It just happened so fast... too fast. They were swept into the portal. The force was too strong."

My heart wanted to console him, to tell him everything would be all right, but that same heart ached for the immensity of my loss. Brax and Moore...

Tears streamed down my cheek.

"But worst of all," Asher went on, "Is losing you. I don't know how I can live with the knowledge that I failed you."

My lips parted and I spoke the words of reassurance and tranquility, but no sound came out. Though I could see his fingers still wrapped around my hand, I could not feel his touch; his warmth. I rose, thinking my subconscious being had taken over, but as I continued to rise, high enough to look down and see Asher kneeling before my limp and bloodied corpse, I knew this was more than a mere loss of consciousness.

I'm here, Asher, I wanted to say, but the words still refused to sound.

A rush of wind blew through my hair and a trail of sparkling dust wafted through the air. The scent of sugar and sweetness tempted my nostrils and suddenly I was carried to another world.

"My dearest, Lux."

The sound of any voice should have alarmed me, but I was soothed and calmed.

"Yes, Lothario." This time my voice resonated loud and strong.

"You've stepped to the other side."

"Have I died?"

"To the mere mortals of this earth, yes. They've lost the human being they'd come to know as Lux."

"My parents…"

"I believe they'll understand what has truly happened to you. They know of your nature. They know of where you've come… and where you should ultimately go. Worry not for them."

I turned to him, my darling guardian angel. "Lothario, have I become immortal?"

"It was not in the plans. This was not how your destiny was to play out."

"But now that I'm here…"

"I know what you will ask."

"Then will you grant me permission?"

"Unfortunately that is something that I cannot do."

"Lothario, they both mean so much to me. They've given so much to fight at my side, to try to keep the demons at bay. I would never have closed the portal without either of them. Please, Lothario, you have to let me go after Moore and Brax."

"I understand all that you owe them, and all that they've done. The outcome of this latest battle saddens me greatly, of that I assure you."

"But…"

"But it is best that you forget about them."

"You know I can't do that. I could never…"

"You are young and resilient. Life will bring new people to you, new experiences, and these will fade away."

"That's lame and you know it. For all the years I've given up having a normal life, for all the sacrifices I've made, this is how I'm compensated? Not even a helping hand in retrieving the young men who've given their very lives to fight demons."

"What do you propose to do, Lux? Enter the portal yourself and go after them?"

"That's exactly what I propose."

A thick mist flowed between us, obscuring my vision of him and bringing a cool breeze. Was this the life of an angel? Was this being immortal?

"Entering the portal could be dangerous, even for one who is immortal. Is this really a risk you want to take? Are you truly prepared to give up what you have on the off chance you save them? Under these conditions, just finding them could prove impossible."

"I have to try, Lothario. No matter how slim the chances, I have to try. What is the use of living eternally if it is to be with the guilt of having let them down?"

"I should have known you wouldn't give up so easily." He grinned and though I knew he didn't want me to go through with this, I could tell he was proud of me nonetheless.

"So you will help me?"

"I can show you how to enter the portal, however greatly that prospect saddens me."

"I've fought through plenty of battles, this last one being the more arduous of all. I'm strong, Lothario, and I think I can do this."

"Hades is not going to be like any battle you've even known. Be prepared for the worst. Be prepared for a fight that will tax you to the limit."

"I will, Lothario."

"This past battle cost you dearly, Lux."

"I know, and I'll keep that in mind."

"You'll be outnumbered like never before."

I nodded, realizing he was trying to get me to change my mind. "Moore and Brax will be there. They'll help me."

"If you can find them."

"They'll help me find them. I trust them, Lothario, and they trust me. No doubt they are already anticipating my arrival. They know I'll do anything to save them."

"Fine, but don't say I didn't give you fair warning."

"I'd never do such a thing."

"The danger now, lies in the reopening of a portal. You'll have to consider the risks involved in opening the same portal again, or attempting to open another more distant one. Either way, you're going to need added protection."

"More than being immortal?" I didn't want to sound naïve, but I would have thought being immortal saved me from… well, mortality.

"Yes," Lothario said, answering my unasked question. "You'll succeed in living on, no matter what happens to you down there, but in what condition and under what circumstances? Satan can easily make eternity a punishment rather than a treasure."

I looked at him, and was moved by the depth of his concern for me. "I realize that."

"In order to give you added protection, you'll need an Angel Mark. It'll save your immortal soul, but it is not something that is easy to come by. If you'll be patient and let me put the wheels in motion, I can help you get one."

I was pleased beyond words. My heartbreak and loss were painful enough without having to constantly question my ability to save myself. With the added protection, I could enter the portal with a greater assurance of victory.

Brax and Moore had disappeared into the portal. It would take superhuman ability to save them now. The sacrifice was immense, but now I'm ready. Reborn. Reclaimed. I was now able to help save them as an angel.

Kailin Gow

"And one more thing," Lothario, my angel from childhood said, "You're not supposed to die yet, Lux. Neither are Brax and Moore. Think what you will about that. It seems you have the advantage of fate on your side. And something all immortals dream of...a second chance."

Lux, Brax, Moore, and Asher's story continues in Book 4 of Beautiful Beings Series

Angel Mark
December 2012

Shadow Light: Beautiful Beings Book 3

What's Coming Up Soon or Now Available

From Bestselling Author Kailin Gow comes

FADE

"My name is Celestra Caine. I am seventeen years old, which makes me a senior at Richmond High. I never thought this would happen to me, but it has... I'm one of those people you see every day, go to school with, remember seeing at the supermarket or the mall, and then one day you don't hear about them any longer. They're gone, and eventually, you forget them."

http://www.kailingowbooks.com/#!__dystopianbooks

Kailin Gow

From Bestselling Author Kailin Gow comes

DESIRE

A Dystopian world where everyone's future is planned out for them at age 18…whether it is what a person desires or not. Kama is about to turn 18 and she thinks her Life's Plan will turn out like her boyfriend's and friend's – as they desired. But when she glimpse a young man who can communicate with her with his thoughts and knows her name…a young man with burning blue eyes and raven hair, who is dressed like no other in her world, she is left to question her Life's Plan and her destiny.

http://www.kailingowbooks.com/#!__dystopianbooks

Want to Know More about *Beautiful Beings*, Author Insight, Author Appearance, Contests and Giveaways?

Join Kailin Gow's Official Facebook Fan Page at:

http://www.facebook.com/KailinGowBooks

Talk to Kailin Gow at:

http://kailingow.wordpress.com

http://www.KailinGowBooks.com

and

on Twitter at: @kailingow